WINDS OF WINTER

A Young Adult Multi-Genre Short Story Collection

BACON AND JONES - HORROR

BAUMAN - COMING OF AGE

DOUGLAS - FAIRYTALES, FOLKLORE, AND MYTHS

HANSCH - GAMELIT   HAWTHORNE - FANTASY

HOBBS - SCI FI ADVENTURE

LAINE AND MONETTE - CONTEMPORARY FICTION

LI BARR - ROMANCE

MEREWETHER - HISTORICAL FICTION

ROBERTS - FANTASY, MYTH AND LEGENDS

RUGOVA - SCI FI DYSTOPIAN

SCARBOROUGH - URBAN FANTASY POETRY

SNOW - COZY MYSTERY

WANDERS - DARK URBAN FANTASY

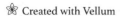 Created with Vellum

CONTENTS

JEFF BACON	Christmas Wrath	1
LOUISA M. BAUMAN	The Mad Girl	19
CORINA DOUGLAS	Rising from the Ashes	39
PARIS HANSCH	An NPC's Christmas	63
LAURA HAWTHORNE	Lost Among Snowflakes	79
H.R. HOBBS	The Blue Pendant	99
REEN JONES	Candy Girl	117
TASCHE LAINE	The Legend of the Glass Stars	133
NOLA LI BARR	Sasha	147
LAUREN LEE MEREWETHER	King's Jubilee	173
JOY MONETTE	The Girl in the Mirror	193
LEIGH ROBERTS	The Outsider	207
A.L. RUGOVA	The Lost Tradition	223
ALICIA SCARBOROUGH	Crimson Eyes	241
MELANIE SNOW	Trouble in Winter Paradise	251
QATARINA WANDERS	Ninth Life	273

CHRISTMAS WRATH

Horror

JEFF BACON

Edited by
Qat Wanders

THE CHRISTMAS CELEBRATIONS WERE OVER. All the family obligations were fulfilled. It was officially winter break. A time for high school friends to get together and catch up on current affairs, revisit first semester college stories, and party.

Lori called me a few days before Christmas with a plan. Her grandfather had died last summer and left a cabin in the mountains to her family. Lori wanted to get the 'old gang' back together, drive up to the secluded cabin, and party for three days. We all agreed and were excited at the opportunity to live parent-free for a few days.

Lori had sweet-talked her dad into letting us take his new Suburban to the cabin. This was good since the roads were snow-packed and icy. The music blared—the sound system was pristine—and we all sang along. Jen had a beautiful voice that put us all to shame. Barb lip-synced and every now and then would bellow out a very flat note. Cam and Jordan were the jocks, they bounced their heads to the music with sunglasses on like they were in a music video. I liked to sing solo, or should I say so low that no one could hear me.

We lost cell signal as we progressed up the mountain. The boys complained because they couldn't upload their 'awesome' videos. They gave Lori a hard time, joking around like they always did. Lori was distracted, having too much fun with Jordan especially to notice the old lady in the middle of the road. She saw the old woman and screamed as the Suburban slammed into her. Lori slammed on her brakes, but it was too late, the truck hit her so hard that she flew fifteen feet and rolled for another ten. The truck slid from side to side and turned completely around; we slid to a stop in the middle of the road.

I opened the door and ran to where the body laid in the

snow. She had to be a hundred years old, crumpled skin, and blood-red eyes. There was blood coming from her mouth, nose, and ears. She reached up to caress my cheek. Her bony fingers embraced my neck, and the palm of her hand was under my ear. She lifted her head as she pulled mine down until her nose touched mine, and with her last breath, she uttered the word "Gryla."

Everyone but Lori got out of the truck and rushed over to the body. They stared in horror; the scene was gruesome. I released the old lady's hand from my neck and laid it down on her chest.

Cam was the first one to have the courage to speak. "Carrie, is—is she dead?"

I checked for a pulse, turned my head up toward Cam. "Yeah, she's dead."

Lori stumbled out of the driver's seat and walked over while trying to call her dad. She was in shock.

Jordan put his arm around Lori to help stabilize her. "No service up here, remember?"

Lori dropped her phone in the snow, "Wha—what— what should we do?"

Barb was the smartest of us all, she was always the one we would go to when we had trouble. She stepped in front of Lori and grabbed both of her hands. "Lori, look at me. Come on, look at me. Where is the nearest phone?"

Lori had locked her eyes onto Barb and was focusing on her versus the lifeless corpse on the side of the road. "The cabin has a phone."

Lori started to come back to reality; the shock was wearing off. She thought for just a minute and continued, "The nearest town is thirty-eight miles away, we are fifteen minutes from the cabin. Our best bet is the cabin."

We all walked to the SUV. Jen stopped, "Hey guys, what about the body?"

Jordan turned around, and his face went blank. "What body?"

Jen thought Jordan was trying to be funny. "The dead body, idiot."

Jordan grabbed Jen's shoulders and turned her around; the body was gone. Only the blood-stained snow remained.

I walked over to where the body had been; there were so many footprints in the snow from all of us, but there were three sets of tracks that went into the woods. The footprints were not made by shoes, but bare feet, and they were very large.

I pleaded with the group, "Guys, get over here, please, now."

They cautiously walked over to where I was standing. I pointed at the large footprints in the snow that led off to the woods.

Barb analyzed the scene. "She must have family up here; they must have taken the body."

Lori flapped her hands as she asked in a wavering voice, "What do we do now?"

Barb replied calmly as if she was in charge, "The plan hasn't changed. We go to the cabin and call the police."

Everyone nodded in agreement. We walked back to the SUV, staring at the blood on the grill of the vehicle. Jordan decided he would take us the rest of the way; Lori was in no shape to drive. Snow had started to fall—the flakes were large and beautiful, but it made driving even more dangerous. Jordan took his time and drove very carefully while Lori gave him directions. It took us thirty minutes, but we finally reached the cabin.

Lori opened the door to the cabin and flipped the switch

to turn on the lights, but nothing happened. She stood there and continued to flip the switch up and down, expecting a different result. Barb went back to the SUV and found a couple flashlights. The rest of us walked into the cabin using the flashlight apps on our cell phones. We searched for the old-fashioned landline phone. Jen found it, but when she picked it up, there was no dial tone.

Jen yelled, "Crap, crap, crap! What do we do now?"

Barb remained calm, "Cam and Jordan, take these flashlights and get some firewood. We'll start a fire for heat. Lori, do you have candles?"

Lori went over to a closet and pulled out a box that contained old newspapers, different-sized candles, and boxes of wooden matches. I saw something on the top shelf of the closet—it was moving, and the eyes reflected the light from my flashlight. I moved toward the closet slowly. Everyone had noticed that I was focused on the closet. As I got to the doorway of the closet, I flashed my light on the top shelf. It was a huge white cat; it jumped off the shelf and ran across the floor.

Jen screamed, "Lori, you have a cat living up here all alone?"

Lori walked over to the cat and began to pet its head. "No, I've never seen this cat before."

Cam was shaking, trying to get a grip on the moment. "Jordan, let's get some firewood so these girls can stop freaking out."

I laughed to myself. Cam's voice was so shaky, yet he was trying to be the big tough guy. He was a good guy. Jordan and Cam opened the door to step outside. The cat followed them out the door. I closed the door behind them.

We could hear the boys clunking the firewood into their arms, but that sound stopped and was replaced with a blood-curdling scream. We all looked out the window to see what was happening. At first, I thought the boys may have been playing a joke on us, but the growls we heard removed that thought from my head.

Jordan ran up to the door while yelling, "Open the door! Open the door!"

Jen opened the door as Jordan ran inside; she slammed the door shut and locked it. She waited by the door for Cam.

Jordan dropped the wood on the floor. "Cam is gone. Something dragged him into the woods." He was bleeding, and there was a large claw mark on his back.

Barb grabbed Jordan's arm. "What was it?"

"I'm not sure. It looked like a mountain lion, but bigger." Jordan fell to the floor with his face in his hands. "Oh God, Cam. I'm sorry, Cam."

Lori walked over and held Jordan as he sobbed. I heard scratching at the door; it was the cat. I walked over to open the door and let it in.

Jen watched me reach for the door lock. "Carrie, don't you open that door."

I opened the door despite Jen's orders. The cat sauntered into the cabin like nothing was wrong with the world. It ran over to where Jordan and Lori were and began to purr while it rubbed up against them.

Lori batted the cat away, "Get away, you creepy cat." But the cat persisted in showing them attention.

Barb had not lost focus on her task. She took the wood, newspapers, and matches and made a fire. She then placed candles around the entire cabin and lit them one by one. The cabin was warming up, and we had just enough light to see.

Barb sat down on the floor. "So, should we stay here

tonight, or should we drive to town?" She was so logical in her thoughts, it was irritating.

I just wanted to have a good panic attack and break down. Jen and I pondered her question while Jordan and Lori continued to cry and hold each other. The sound of a tree breaking followed by a large crash, breaking glass, and a thud came from outside. We ran to the window to see what had happened. A large tree had fallen on the SUV. The tree had come down with such force that the truck was wrapped around the tree. The wheels were driven into the ground.

The choice was made for us: we were staying at the cabin.

Barb, Jen, and I sat down by Lori and Jordan, the cat was sitting on Jordan's lap as it watched us.

Lori rocked back and forth as she watched the flames dance in the fireplace. She cleared her throat, "Grandpa would never let us come up here after Christmas. I begged him to come up here, but he would always say the cabin was shut down for the holidays."

Barb slanted her head as she looked at Lori. "How long has your family owned this cabin?"

Lori continued to stare at the fire. "This was the original homestead; this land has been in our family for over three hundred years."

I was impressed. "That's incredible, but you never spent a Christmas up here?"

Lori took a deep breath. "Grandpa used to tell me a story about these mountains."

Jen played with the warm wax from a candle. "Well, tell us the story."

Lori cleared her throat again; she was nervous. "These

mountains were the home to a witch and her husband. The witch's name was Gryla—"

I raised my head. "Wait, did you say Gryla?"

Lori partially squinted her eyes at me, "Yeah, Gryla. Why? Have you heard this story?"

I started to shake my head. "That was the last word the old woman said to me before she died: Gryla."

All eyes were focused on me; it was uncomfortable. They looked at me like this was important information that I should have shared.

Lori slowly nodded her head as she looked down at the floor. She continued her story. "There was a terrible snow storm that lasted for weeks. Gryla, her husband, and thirteen children were stranded on the mountain. Two days before Christmas, they ran out of food, but they couldn't go out to hunt nor could they make it to the nearest town. They were set to starve."

Jen was hanging on every word Lori spoke. "Did they die of starvation?"

Lori calmly responded, "No. Gryla made the choice between her beloved husband and hungry children. She melted snow into a large pot, then killed her husband and made a stew out of his body."

Barb was aghast. "Oh my God, that's disgusting."

"Well, her husband was also a magical being. With his last breath, he cursed his body. Anyone who ate his flesh was doomed to walk the mountain for all eternity without form."

"Without form—what does that mean? Ghosts?" I blurted out the question without thinking. I was hooked on the story.

Lori put her hand on the cat's head and gave it a good

scratch. "The curse didn't work that way, the children all became shape-shifters. They became known as the Yule Lads. Gryla was given immortality. They had a cat they called the Yule Cat—it was a scroungy mongrel. It also became a shape-shifter, but could only change into different types of cats."

Jen was agitated. "So, is that it? Gryla and her family live up here for eternity—the end?"

Lori smiled as she continued to pet the cat. "No, the legend continues that the curse restricted Gryla, the Yule Lads, and Yule Cat. They are only permitted to leave the cave they lived in for thirteen days, one for each child. Those thirteen days start on Christmas Day. The legend states the family will go out and hunt for naughty children, rotten parents, and anyone they deemed to be evil. That is the only thing they are permitted to eat, and they only have those few days to gather enough food to make it through the rest of the year."

Barb stood up. "Wow, that's a really good story—bad Christmas story—would be better if it was set around Halloween. I gotta pee."

Barb picked up one of the candles off a table and slowly walked to the bathroom and shut the door. Jordan was abnormally quiet, but it seemed reasonable considering everything he had been through that night. I kept staring at the cat, I was imagining that it was the 'Yule Cat' who had come for us, and it was just waiting for the right moment to strike. I laughed at the absurd thought.

The sound of a window breaking came from the bathroom, followed by screams of pain from Barb. Jen and I sprung off the floor and ran over to the bathroom door. Barb had locked it. We threw our shoulders into the door as we tried to break in. Barb's screams became gurgled and fainter as we continued to beat on the door. The door jamb finally gave way—the door flung open. There was blood on every wall, but it was concentrated by the window. Clumps of hair stuck to the wall, it looked like Barb's body was pulled through the broken window.

I pushed Jen out of the bathroom and slammed the door shut. I turned around to see Jordan thrusting a knife into Lori's chest. Her body dropped to the floor as the blood gushed from it. Her eyes were fixed on me as her head jerked violently while she died. I tried to run to her, but Jordan backhanded me, and I tripped, landing on the couch. I looked up and saw that cat perched on the kitchen counter as it watched us.

I rubbed my cheek. "What the hell, Jordan?"

Jen was sitting on the floor staring at Lori's body as she cried.

Jordan turned so I could see his face. His pupils were rolled to the back of his head, and all I could see were the whites of his eyes. He straightened up and adjusted his shirt like he was preparing for a formal meeting.

"You have to choose. We're willing to let one of you live, the other must walk out that door."

I grabbed a candlestick as I rushed over to Jordan. He took another swing at me but missed. I smacked his head with the candlestick. He grabbed me by the shoulders and pulled me down as he thrusted his knee into my stomach. I fell to the floor as I tried to catch my breath.

Jen mumbled, "Why, Jordan? Why?"

"Jordan's not here right now, it's just us. Stop resisting and just choose."

I looked up and could see blood running down the side of his face. There was nothing familiar about him. Jordan was gone and something was using his body. I was in survival mode. *If he can bleed, we can stop him.*

I walked over to where Jen was sitting, I brushed the hair out of her face, grabbed her hand, and helped her stand to her feet. I looked over to the corner where there were two ski poles. She looked at the corner then back at me and very gently nodded. She understood what I was thinking.

I walked around the back of Jen to maneuver closer to the poles. "Why can't you just let us go? Why does someone have to die?"

Jordan's voice was gruff, "We do not bargain. Choose now."

I was close enough to grab the ski poles. I threw one to Jen, and we ran at Jordan with them. I stuck mine in his upper stomach while Jen stuck hers in Jordan's neck. We pushed him up against a wall and continued to stab at him until he fell to the ground, lifeless. We had just killed Jordan, or what used to be Jordan.

Jen's body shook as she slammed her fist on the back of a chair. "What do we do now?"

"We need to stay calm, stay in the main part of the cabin, and wait for help. Someone will come here looking for us in a couple days. We just need to stay in the cabin."

Jen paced the floor as she played with the zipper on her sweatshirt. "What about the fire? How do we keep it going so we don't freeze?"

"We burn the furniture. We can stay here for at least a week as long as we are smart."

We didn't notice the cat was listening to our conversation. It jumped off the counter, looked at us, and hissed, then strutted to the middle of the room and growled. The growling became louder and more pronounced as its body began to change. We watched in horror as this small cat became as big as a tiger. The process looked painful; the cat's face and mannerisms looked miserable while it shifted.

Jen and I ran into the bedroom and locked the door. We pushed every piece of furniture in the bedroom up against the door. We heard glass breaking, furniture crashing up against the walls—the cabin was being torn apart—we could feel the waves of destruction through the wall. Then we heard a whoosh and could smell the smoke building in the air; the cabin was on fire.

We pushed the furniture out of the way and opened the door. The cat was gone, but the cabin was on fire. There was a path to the front door; we needed to get out immediately.

"Jen, we need to make a break for the door, then run into the woods. It's our only hope."

Jen nodded, and we sprinted toward the door. We made it outside only to be surrounded by thirteen ogre-sized men and one hungry-looking Yule Cat. We turned to run back into the cabin, but we were not fast enough. The Yule Lads caught us, threw us down on the ground and put us into large burlap bags. I couldn't see what was happening, but I knew I was riding on someone's shoulder, being hauled up the mountain. I could hear Jen screaming; then I heard a thud, and the screaming stopped. I didn't know what happened to Jen but knew enough to keep my mouth shut.

It felt like we were walking up the mountain. I could feel the cold air coming through the burlap with every gust of wind. The wind stopped, and I was dropped down on the ground. The top of the bag was ripped open, and I was grabbed by the hair and guided to a table where I was tied down with leather straps. I looked over to see Jen was strapped to another table in the same manner. She looked alive but unconscious.

Two of the Yule Lads came over to the foot of the tables. They pulled out little bags from their pockets and poured black stones into their hands. They showed each other their rocks; there was one white rock and several black rocks. They both threw the rocks in the air above their respective table. The rocks landed on my body—the white rock landed on my chest.

The men took the straps off Jen and hauled her out of the cave. I heard a couple of screams, then nothing. I knew I was next. I never imagined this is how I would die. The men came back and took the straps off me. I tried to run away, but they were too strong. One of them slapped me across the face, which dazed me just enough to allow them to drag me further into the cave.

We went deeper and deeper into the cave until we arrived at some sort of shrine. It looked satanic, with torches lit all around the chamber. There was a rack of sorts in the middle of the room. I was hauled to that rack where my legs, arms, and head were bound to it. The part that my head was strapped to tilted and swiveled so I could look around the room.

There were several idols carved from stalagmites surrounding the rack. One of the men came over and grabbed my head and bent it backward. There was something metal shoved into my mouth and a warm liquid was poured down my throat. They plugged my nose; I had no choice but to swallow. I held out as long as I could, but I eventually swallowed it all.

Then men released my head, stood in a circle, and started chanting. I couldn't make out what they were saying; it sounded like they were speaking in Latin. The room was spinning; I was having a hard time staying conscious.

I heard a voice in my head. "Relax, my dear. I'm going to join you, then everything will be right as rain."

It was a calm, motherly voice; it made me feel like everything was going to be all right, but I knew it was not. I felt like I was falling into a bottomless pit. Everything was getting smaller, like I was a great distance from the reality I saw through my eyes. I landed and was standing in a black room. I looked up and could see through my eyes like I would a big-screen television.

I could see one of the Lads come up and untie my body. He brushed my hair behind my ear and looked at me with love.

"Mother, is that you?"

I yelled, "No, I'm not your mother! Let me go!"

But I heard my voice say, "Yes, my children, I am back. Prepare the other girl's body for stew. We need to eat before we hunt."

I fell to my knees and started to cry. The motherly voice spoke like she had a loudspeaker system in this hell.

"There, there, child, I am Gryla. We will be together for quite some time. It is nice to have another woman to talk to."

I watched as the Lads deboned Jen and threw her body into the pot. They took the bones and put them into a bucket. My body stood over the pot and hummed, putting ingredients into the pot. The Yule Cat came over, and my body threw it a piece of Jen's corpse. It rubbed up against my leg and purred. This was my fate. I was a prisoner in my own body. I could only watch and listen.

Gryla spoke to me, "Oh, come dear, it's not that bad. We have each other for the rest of your life."

ABOUT THE AUTHOR

Jeff Bacon was born and raised on a farm near the city of Aberdeen, South Dakota. He now lives in Janesville, Wisconsin with his wife, their children, and 2 dogs. Jeff writes in the Dark Fantasy, Urban Fantasy, and Horror genres. Check out his website or social media pages for more information and upcoming releases.

www.jbchivvy.com

Facebook: @jbaconauthor
Instagram: @realbaconjeff

THE MAD GIRL

Coming of Age

LOUISA M. BAUMAN

IF I WERE as perfect as my sister, I'd have a pretty boring life. While she's sitting at home completing her homework and studying for tests, I'm outside having crazy adventures with my friends. I don't study because once I've learned something, I never forget it. I'm at the top of my class and that's where I want to be, but for some reason, my family still doesn't love me. When I mention my high grades without having studied, I can see and feel the hostility seeping from their eyes.

"Pride goes before a fall," Mom says on behalf of the family, as if they hope I do fall and smash my brains in the process, bringing me down to the level where they think I belong. I often score 100% on my tests, and it never ceases to give me a shot of adrenaline on top of my sense of accomplishment. But the sad thing is, I want love most of all, yet it's so much easier for me to be intelligent than to be lovable. In my antiquated town of Victoria, which is located smack in the middle of vast acres of farm fields, the citizens have this old-school notion that sweet submissiveness and humbleness are still the most desirable traits for a young woman to have.

Is it my fault that I missed out on both attributes when the creator was doling out personalities? I have a hard time accepting my flaws, but in spite of that, I do have dozens of friends. My parents don't approve of most of my friends, but I think that's because they never liked their parents from when they were young. At least my friends are fun to be with.

The church ladies, especially my mom's four sisters, stare at me askance whenever I do or say anything contrary to their preconceived notions of propriety. Their eyes glittering, they whisper to my mother that she ought to control that reckless daughter of hers. My mom clenches her jaw and her eyes flash as she lets out a big huff of exasperation. I'd respect my mother if she defended me once in a while against her sisters' allegations, but it's plain to see she wants to please them and she doesn't care about me.

"Do you think I haven't tried?"

How do I know they're gossiping about me and exaggerating my harmless (to me) escapades? Because they *always* exaggerate. Also, I have a secret power. Call it intuition, or call it sixth sense, but I just know stuff. Maybe it's because I listen to and trust that little voice inside my head, or maybe I'm just ultra sensitive to the tiny clues around me. Sometimes I even know what will happen in the future, although I don't tell anyone. I don't want to be a freak. Besides, nobody would believe me. But it gives me such secret satisfaction when I'm right.

I watch my sister as she studies; she's hunched over her pile of textbooks, her forehead wrinkled and her lips moving. And I know, despite all her studying, that she will barely pass. Not that it takes any superpower to know that. She goes into panic mode during tests and writes wrong answers to questions she knows very well, but her mind freezes. Yet she will get more praise from my mom for her lousy mark than I will get for my high grade, this I also know. Because she loves my sister more than she loves me.

December has arrived in Ontario, Canada, and that means winter is upon our doorstep. Most people grumble when the temperature drops, but not me. I revel in this season and I think it's because the coldness fits my nature so well. Or maybe it's because I like how everything smells fresh and clean and pure outdoors. Hot summer days kill me unless I'm under water, which I do as often as possible.

The main street in our little town is already dressed in festive gear—wreaths hanging from the lamp poles, Christmas lights twinkling from the eaves, Santa Claus displays on every lawn, and jaunty holiday music blaring from every shop and street corner. I'd love to do my Christmas shopping in the city and buy great gifts for my family and friends, but my mom thinks that's frivolous and won't let me go. She wants me to do home baking or crafts instead, but who wants my homemade crap?

I'm sixteen now and she still doesn't trust me to do anything right. We argue a lot. Sometimes I try to become the kind, sweet person she wants me to be, but it never lasts long. I ignore the dark blots on my soul and convince myself that I *am* capable of being a daughter any mother would be proud of.

In fact, today I'm having one of those days when I want to prove myself, but it's only nine in the morning and I'm already dying inside. Dying. I'm sitting on the couch like a good girl, cradling the family cat in my lap, and reading a murder mystery in between ruminating about my life. The outlook is grim. Either I transform myself into the person my mother wants me to be, or I rebel and remain forever in conflict with her and the rest of my family. I do love to read and the average book takes me only three hours to read. If I read inspirational books all day, I might have a tiny chance of becoming a lovable girl, but the rough books I love to read make me thirst for adventure rather than tame my inner monster.

Mom doesn't approve of me reading books with guns and shooting, so she brings me Christian books on love and forgiveness. I read them and I even agree with some of them, but they are impossible to put into practice. Mom keeps watching me after I read these character-building books and makes it painfully obvious she's praying for a miracle to happen. Maybe the books will do the job she is unable to do.

For example, one day I refused to babysit my younger siblings because I had previously planned to do something with my friends.

"They're not my kids. You made them; you babysit them. I'm not going to."

Mom grits her teeth. "Oh you pig-headed thing! Do you think Elsie Dinsmore would talk back to her mother like you do?"

"Elsie Dinsmore is not a real person, so she doesn't count."

"What about your friends? Do you think Nancy and Mary are as disrespectful to their mother as you are?"

"Just leave me alone!" I scream, stamping my foot. The red-hot monster inside me explodes in a fire of profanity and violent words. My sister and my brothers grin from the sidelines, enjoying the show and patting themselves on the back that they are good kids and not evil like me. God, I hate them all.

I run to my room and slam the door. I flop on the bed facedown, grab the bag of Doritos hidden under the bed and read my murder book. I block out the infuriating expectations my family sets upon me. My siblings bang on my door, only because they know I want to be left alone.

"Doris is mad and I am glad, and I know how to please her," they taunt on the other side of the door. I oblige them with a murderous string of words that ought to burn their ears off.

"Leave the mad thing alone," I hear Mom say, and eventually they leave, chanting the stupid rhyme. One day, I am going to get even.

'Vengeance is mine, says the Lord.' I don't want those words to enter my consciousness. I want to wreak the worst possible revenge on the entire world for refusing to understand me.

Then inexplicably, on my sixteenth birthday, my mother gives me the rare diamonds passed down from her grandmother. I have long admired and coveted these gems but didn't expect to ever possess them while my mother was alive.

"You're an adult now," she says, as if diamonds and the dawn of another day have the ability to transform my rebellious character into a pleasant one. "I trust you to be responsible with this priceless heirloom, and in exchange I want you to behave like a mature adult."

"I will, I will," I say, my eyes glittering to match the diamonds. I mean it too, with all my heart. "Thank you, Mom." I take the jewels out of her hand before she changes her mind. She quickly suppresses the glare that flares in her eyes, and I know she already knows that these diamonds can't bring about the hoped-for magic transformation. Secretly, I despise her for trying to buy her way into my affections, but I go along with it because I am shallow enough to want and enjoy new things. The diamonds are the best thing she has ever given me, and I decide to surprise her and become a perfect daughter, like my younger sister.

"These diamonds come with a great responsibility," Mom says. I roll my eyes. I hate when she gives me long lectures and I feel one coming my way. "These diamonds have been passed down in my family for centuries. Traditionally, the eldest daughter of the family always receives them on her sixteenth birthday. According to legend, if this custom is not continued, the entire Macdonald clan will suffer financially, physically and emotionally and be ultimately destroyed. If the diamonds are lost, stolen, or sold, someone in the family will die every day until they are restored to the proper owner."

My mother's eyes stray to the diamonds resting in my palm. I shiver. The diamonds lose some of their shine. She didn't give them to me out of love, but out of obligation. She gave them to me only because she didn't want all the Macdonalds to point their fingers at her and blame her for every misfortune and every death that befell them from this day forth.

"Why did you never tell us this story before, Mom?"

"You didn't need to know, Doris. This is a tremendous responsibility to sit upon your shoulders and I wanted you to be carefree a little longer."

Carefree. Wow. Moms are so out of touch with the life and trials of youth. Still, she has a point. I already feel burdened with these stones but there is nothing I can do to escape my destiny.

Now, a day later, I shift on the couch and reach into my jeans pocket. The diamonds should be locked up in the safe, I know, and I will put them back there after I've admired them one more time. Or two times. I have decided to ignore the family legend for now and pretend these diamonds are just ordinary diamonds made purely for *my* pleasure and nothing else. The story could easily be just some old wives' tale.

My fingers grasp the finely crafted cloth purse that contains the dazzling jewels. The diamonds must be worth at least a million dollars. I shake them into my hand. Each glittering gem is the size of a robin's egg. I admire how the sunshine sparkles upon them and wonder if my life will improve now that I'm sixteen years old and the owner of two fabulous diamonds. My sister looks up from her textbooks and narrows her eyes.

"You don't deserve those diamonds."

"I deserve them. I have to put up with you and the rest of the brats in this family." I drop my treasure back into the cloth purse and stuff them deep into my pocket, away from the prying eyes of my perfect sister. Her eyes grow dark and her lips turn downward as she turns back to her homework.

Then I remember that it's be-nice-to-your-family day. "I'm sorry, Diane. I didn't mean that. You're not a brat; you're a very nice sister." I smile kindly and try to be happy for her that she has a sweet personality, even though I don't. But I'm the one that got the diamonds. For once I'm glad I'm the oldest daughter of this family.

"Put them in the safe," she murmurs.

"I will, as soon as I go back upstairs. Don't worry. They are fine in my pocket."

An hour goes by and all is well. My veneer is still sticking, mainly because nobody is home except for me and my perfect sister. I'm almost at the end of the second last chapter of my book when there's a knock on the door. I toss the book on the couch and get up. Snarky rolls off my lap, twists, and lands with four feet on the floor. She shakes her whiskers at me, not too happy about being startled out of her sleep.

"Sarah! What a surprise!" Maybe my bestie will help me put everything into perspective.

"Hey Doris, are you busy?"

"Nope, not at all. What's up?"

"I'm helping Dad clean up the horse chestnuts under our tree. We're almost done, and then we're going to take them back to the bush with the tractor and dump them. Wanna come?"

"I sure do. I'm exploding with perfection and I can't stand it another minute."

Sarah's snorted. "I wouldn't use you and perfection in one sentence, my friend."

"Your lack of confidence in my character is disturbing. Listen, I'm turning over a new leaf now that I'm sixteen and I *am* going to become a perfect daughter. I need your support, not your doubts."

Sarah backs away in mock horror. Her round brown eyes sparkle with mischief as usual, and that curl of dark hair springing from her widow's peak adds to her naughty elfin look. "You need more than support, hun. You need a miracle."

"Thanks."

"Come on over with me and when we're done with the chestnuts, we'll hike in the forest one last time before the snow flies."

"Sounds like a plan." I grab my jacket, feeling less stressed already. I turn around and shout. "Diane, I'm leaving!"

My sister grumbles something I don't understand and I head outdoors. Snarky slips through the door before I can close it, so I let her come along. She's too smart to run away from me; I'm her food supplier.

On the way over to Sarah's house, I show her the diamonds but I don't tell her the legend attached to them. I want her to think my mom gave them to me only because she loves me, with no strings attached. Sarah oohs and aahs over the little beauties, then I shove them deep into my jeans pocket again. Sarah can't believe I'm carrying them with me, but I'm sure it's okay.

Sarah and her dad are not nearly finished cleaning up the messy chestnuts, and I become suspicious of Sarah's motives in luring me to her house. She hands me a pair of gloves. I raise my eyebrows without comment, put on the gloves, and help her scoop chestnuts into the bucket of the tractor. Sarah's sassy smile and her corny jokes make up for the backbreaking labor I've been tricked into, and I don't mind helping out. Her dad is just as funny as Sarah is and he's a big tease.

When I'm around Sarah, getting my hands dirty doesn't seem so terrible. Not like at home when I'd scream blue murder and call up the kids helpline if I were forced to do such demeaning work. But at Sarah's house it's different and actually kind of fun.

In no time at all, we're done. Sarah and I hitch a ride on the tractor and we putt-a-putt back to the bush, where we dump the nuts for the squirrels to munch on. It's easy food for them to tuck away for the winter. I hold Snarky in my arms and she peers about with interest, her ears and her nose twitching constantly as she tries to watch everything in all directions at once.

Sarah's dad dumps little piles of nuts in different locations throughout the woods while Sarah and I follow on foot. A mouse scurries from beneath a bush. Snarky pounces on the creature with her claws extended and that is the end of the mouse. Snarky carries the limp creature in her jaws, the gray thread of a tail and two hind legs dangling from one side, and the head and tiny forepaws from the other.

Most of the leaves have fallen off the branches and lie in a thick carpet on the ground. The few stragglers on the trees look mighty lonely and fragile. Sarah and I find a huge rock to stand on and we use pieces of broken branches as a microphone. Her dad is now leaving us to our fun and waves good-bye from the seat of his tractor.

"Rock it, Baaay...bie...! Standing-upon-a rock, baay...bee!"

We laugh our heads off while we invent song lyrics and dance for the trees, our esteemed audience. Our laughter echoes through the woods and floats away on the clouds.

On the way home from Sarah's house at dusk, I remember the diamonds and reach into my pocket to touch them. I reach into the other pocket. My fingers scratch every corner of both pockets, but they aren't there. They. Are. Gone.

I race back to the woods, my breath coming in gasps. Twilight is upon me and I must find them. Now, before somebody dies. If my mom discovers I lost them, even for a moment, she will kill me. And I'll help her. If someone must die because of my carelessness, it better be me.

Here is one more black mark against me for even leaving the house with the diamonds. The blackest of black marks possible. Worse than losing a priceless heirloom is the thought of my shame and the family's further derision of my character. Do they think I *want* to be responsible for a family member's death? I run into the woods, praying that a divine hand directs me to the right spot. The black branches of the trees close in on me in sinister threats and the leaf stragglers are demons ready to descend upon me in flecks of ill omens.

The temperature is dropping. As I drop to my knees in the area by the rock we'd danced upon, the first snowflakes fall. I scrabble and scrunch through the leaves, ignoring my cold fingers as I search for the proverbial needle in a haystack. What if the cursed things are buried beneath a pile of nuts? If I don't find the diamonds, I am going to kill myself. So much for becoming the perfect daughter. I might have known it would never happen.

I consider going back to Sarah's house for the night but I quickly discard that idea. Her dad will insist on 'doing the right thing' and call my mom about my whereabouts. And then she'll freak out about the missing diamonds. More snow falls, as if mother nature herself is ashamed of me and is trying to cover my evil with her pure white crystals. I'll have to find a cave to sleep in, if there is one in these woods. There has to be. In novels there is always a cave in the woods for lost people and surely these woods are no different. Not that Sarah has ever mentioned any cave in this forest and her family owns it. But it could be a cave that nobody knows about yet and I'll become famous for discovering it. I give up the search for the diamonds and search for a cave instead.

Oh, and berries. I better watch out for berry bushes. Every forest in every survival book I've ever read has berry bushes to feed the hungry wanderer. This is just a fact of life. Forests contain berry bushes. Usually in books, the heroes have an axe with them, some matches, and food. But I have nothing except the clothes on my back. I check my jeans pocket to be sure. Nothing. Not even a tissue or a pack of gum.

I'm still looking for a cave and berry bushes when night blots out my vision and I quit my groping around and just sit down on the ground right where I am. I remind myself that I am a smart girl and this adventure is all in a day's work for me, nothing to get upset about.

Will they worry about me, send a search party, or invent a story about me moving out of the country? Maybe they're all on their knees praying that I've been murdered so they no longer have to deal with me. But if the diamonds are lost, the Macdonalds are done for. Every day one of the clan will die until they are all wiped out. It's a terrible situation.

I rest my back against the tree and ignore the cold and discomfort. I'm not going to die of exposure in one night. Yes, the ground is frosty, and I'm extremely cold and uncomfortable, but it won't kill me. All I need is to get through one minute at a time. Anything is better than going home without the diamonds. I don't need to be reminded how stupid I was to carry them around in my pocket, and in a forest carpeted with fallen leaves, no less. Well what's done is done and I will find the stupid stones as soon as day breaks, or die trying.

I drowse but don't fall asleep completely. I hold my arms around myself but it doesn't stop me from shivering. I dream disconnected things about my perfect sister, night creatures and diamonds. Nothing makes sense. Coyotes howl in the distance and I can't believe how much they sound like crying children. I stop panic in its tracks. Coyotes don't attack people. Coyotes are afraid of people and won't get close to them unless they are very sick. There have been no rabid coyotes reported in this area. I will not be attacked by these coyotes.

"Aaaaahhh!" Something scratches at my ankles with sharp claws. I leap to my feet and spin in circles not knowing which way I should run. If a rabid animal touches me with its saliva, I could die.

"Meouw."

My cat. I let my shoulders slump. Well. In my distress, I completely forgot about Snarky. It seems I have at least one faithful friend left in the world. I sweep the darkness for the glow of feline eyes but I can't see her.

"Meouw." I reach out to touch her and my fingers brush

her whiskers. It is totally pitch dark out here. Is this what it's like for blind people? My hand connects with something soft and furry hanging from her mouth.

"EEKK!! Take that thing away!" I don't usually slap my cat, but I can't allow her to drop a dead mouse in my lap. It goes flying into the void. I understand about the rules of nature, but I seriously don't want the evidence dropped in my lap like that. I reach for Snarky and take her into my lap.

"Sorry for hitting you, Snarky. Please forgive me." I stroke her soft fur and try to cuddle her, but she's acting weird and doesn't want to relax. Is she really mad at me? There's no way I'm going to release her though, now that I've found another familiar living body. I fall asleep with the cat squirming restlessly.

When morning comes, my limbs are frozen and stiff, but I pry myself off the ground and get up. The search must continue. If a Macdonald dies today, who will it be? Me? I shudder. Or Grandpa Macdonald in the nursing home? My cousin Jen's newborn baby? One of my siblings? Why doesn't that thought make me feel better? All they ever do is annoy me, but they are my family. We share the same parents, the same house, the same bloodline. They are a part of me and one day they will surely grow up and stop being so annoying. Diane is not so bad. There is something to be said for perfection, really. Perfect people are easy to have around, but only if you don't become jealous of them. It's not Diane's fault that she's a good daughter and not her fault that I am jealous of her. Yes, I am the problem.

All of a sudden, I really, really miss my family. I'm so afraid one of them will die before I find the diamonds. Should I go and get help? I search the frost-covered ground, praying I will find the diamonds soon. Snarky is nowhere to be seen, and probably she's gone hunting again. She'd make a better barn cat than a house cat. I never cry and so I don't understand why I suddenly discover frozen rivulets of ice running down my cheeks. My belly rumbles and my throat feels parched. There are no berries. Could I eat raw horse chestnuts? If I had something with which to build a fire, I could roast them.

I catch a glimpse of Snarky out of the corner of my eye, and yes, there is something hanging from her mouth. I sigh and accept it. Cats will catch mice when they are hungry and lost in the woods. She drops it beside me and I scootch away from it. Snarky claws me on the arm.

"Ouch! What is wrong with you? Don't you dare go feral on me, Snarky!" I glare at her. "And take that . . . !" I stare at the ground. Can it be? CAN IT BE? I grab the prize Snarky has brought me and press it to my heart. Two rock hard nuggets dig into the soft flesh of my breast through the soft material of the purse and I do a happy dance with tears streaming down my cheeks. I grab my cat and bury my face in her fur. This time she doesn't struggle, but purrs, her body vibrating like it always does when she's happy.

"Snarky, we're going home! Home to our family where we belong. Let's go!"

I race along the frozen, rutted path out of the woods to the roadway. Snarky follows closely and a couple of times I almost trip over her. It's snowing again, and I stick out my tongue to catch the moisture. My mother opens the door when she sees me running towards the house.

"Doris! Where have you been? You look half frozen."

"No, I'm not frozen. I feel warmer than I have in a long time."

"Ok, dear. Come inside and get ready to go to the funeral home. Grandpa Macdonald died in his sleep last night and we're all going over there."

I stop short and swallow hard. "Yes, Mom."

She gives me a strange look as I wrap my arms around her in a big hug, then enter the house. I smile a bittersweet smile and wonder when I last hugged her spontaneously like that, or said, 'Yes, Mom' without arguing.

ABOUT THE AUTHOR

Louisa M. Bauman writes from her hermit zone, an apartment in Brampton, Ontario. She is a life-long learner who is fascinated by past events and how those events have helped shape the present and the future. In between the heavier research-based writing, she writes light-hearted short stories to remind herself that she still has a sense of humor. She is the author of historical fiction novels *Sword of Peace* and *Sister, Fight Valiantly* as well as a children's book *The True Story of a Lamb*.

www.louisambaumanauthor.com

Facebook: @Louisa M Bauman
Twitter: @Auntblacksheep
Instagram: @louisambauman

RISING FROM THE ASHES

Fairytales, Folklore, and Myths

CORINA DOUGLAS

Edited by
Joy Sephton

Fergus, the leader of the Institute, turned his gaze to the door. "Reuben, thank you for coming on such short notice."

Grandfather ignored the pleasantries. "Why, Fergus? I understood the boy hasn't hurt anyone."

"Not yet, but he's burnt down Seraph's lab. He's volatile, and that means he's dangerous."

I jerked in my seat, the magical bindings on my wrists burning.

"Something to say to that, Gage?" Fergus inquired.

I glared at him. I just wanted to get out of here. Fortunately, having Reuben here would accelerate the process for I was his protégé, and he needed me.

"He is prophesied, Fergus." Grandfather's words were sharp. "We all need to support him."

A stony glare came over Fergus's face. "No, we don't. The law's clear. The Institute stands outside prophecy."

I'd heard the words many times before. The Masters gave it to me every time I stepped out of line. They disliked me intensely. However, their dislike had turned to fear after I'd burned down Seraph's lab. The truth was, they were right to feel it; I knew how little control I had.

Grandfather's brows snapped together. "That's rubbish! By not supporting him, you're taking a goddamned side! You're letting *him* win!"

Fergus stiffened. "I refuse to get into a debate about the prophecy. Until our laws change, our stance remains the same. The boy will continue to be treated like everyone else."

A muscle ticked in Grandfather's jaw. "Fine! That debate won't end anytime soon," he relented. "But I want to know why Gage was alone in the lab. Surely Seraph had mechanisms in place to prevent entry outside of hours? If you ask me, the blame should equally be laid on Seraph's shoulders, and it definitely doesn't warrant my grandson being suspended!"

Fergus opened his mouth to reply, but there was a knock at the door, and two people were ushered in.

My breath froze in my chest. I recognized them immediately.

The woman had fine lines marring her skin, but she was still beautiful and impeccably dressed. She'd taken the room in at a glance, her expression arranged to her advantage.

The man by her side was a few years older, his skin sunken and sallow, the spark dead in his eyes. I clenched my teeth, fully aware that he'd been beaten by his own demons.

The woman spoke first. "Gage! My baby, are you alright?"

It was as if the last eleven years had never been.

"Get out!" I snapped coldly.

The heat was gathering inside, the pressure building. I felt perspiration break across my forehead as I fought to retain control, pushing the old memories away. This couldn't happen again, not here, not now.

Reuben sensed the change immediately, moving to stand beside me. One of his large hands dropped onto my shoulder, squeezing hard. "Danielle, Steven, there's no need for you to be here. Gage is my responsibility."

My father stiffened. "We were called in. We heard he's destroyed a building." His eyes were haunted as he added, "It's not the first time this has happened."

An inferno was building inside me, my father's words another trigger. Reuben squeezed my shoulder again, his fingers biting deep into the tissue. It hurt, but it pierced the veil of my emotions and shifted my focus to that one place.

Danielle laughed. "I'm surprised you remember, Steven!"

I bit my lip, fighting the urge to scream.

"Enough!" Rueben roared. "This is not about you!" He turned to Fergus. "Why are they even here? I'm Gage's first point of contact."

Fergus clasped his hands together in the folds of his robe. "Because Gage needs somewhere to stay. As a result of his actions, he will be leaving the Institute."

Danielle gasped. "He's being expelled?"

"No; rather a suspension. Gage shows promise to be one of the most powerful Druids we've ever had; however, he battles with control. The first few years of study are the toughest, and we expect a tolerable level of accidents, but Gage is sixteen now, and he's still struggling. This must be remedied immediately. If he fails to attain control, we'll have no choice but to expel him."

A hushed silence fell over the room. Being expelled meant my magic would be revoked. It was inconceivable. My magic was an integral part of who I was. Without it, I wouldn't be whole, not after losing my brother.

"Gage will be taking a leave of absence from the Institute for three months," Fergus continued. "During this time, it's expected that he'll work on his control. I'll send a Master to assess him for suitability at the end of the tenure. If he shows improvement, he'll be accepted back in."

My stomach dropped. *If* I was accepted back in.

"This doesn't make any sense!" my father burst out. "Someone has to have complained. I don't remember a student being suspended for an accident!" I saw his fists clench with aggression. "It was Creag, wasn't it? He's been financially supporting the Institute for years. It's no secret he's wanted one over me since Danielle chose me instead of him!"

Fergus's face darkened. "I don't respond to influence, Steven. Druidic lore alone guides me."

The reprimand was firm, with enough conviction that my father turned away.

Danielle cleared her throat. "Unfortunately, I can't help. My mother requires my full attention."

Reuben's voice was mocking. "Still running with that story, Danielle?"

She flushed. "She's bedridden. I can't leave her side."

"So that's why you're here now?" Steven queried mildly.

Danielle sneered at him. "And I suppose you think you're capable of looking after Gage yourself then?"

It was happening again. I didn't need this. "Stop it! I'm not going with either of you!"

"That's right," Reuben interjected firmly. "Gage belongs with me. You two are incapable." He turned to Fergus, adding, "I'll ensure he gets all the support he needs."

"I agree," Fergus replied swiftly, palpable relief peppering his tone. "Give me a half-hour, and he'll be ready for release."

The ride home was quiet. Reuben didn't try to fill the silence.

I sat there, numb from the encounter with my parents. I hadn't seen them since that fateful night. I hadn't meant to burn down Seraph's lab, just like I hadn't meant to burn down the family home.

In the quiet, that memory crowded in. I fought it, like so many times before; trying to push it into a dark corner of my mind and slam a lid on it. But it refused to be ignored. Seeing my parents again for the first time since that event was too much of a catalyst, and in the quiet of the car, the past broke through my barriers, and I relived the moment that irrevocably changed my life.

Father had come home early that night, one fish his only catch for the day.

"I'm sick to death of fish!" Mother cried.

He turned to her, a slight sway to his movements. "Come on, Dani," he cajoled. "It's only for tonight. My catch will be better tomorrow."

"The only thing guaranteed tomorrow is that any profit you make, you'll be drinking from a bottle!" She shook her head. "I'm sick of pretending to be happy with the lot you've given me!"

My insides twisted. She'd confirmed what I'd always believed: she didn't want us. But it was Father's face that caught my attention, his expression taut.

"What are you saying, Dani?"

Mother's face blanched, but she held her ground. "I want out, Steven."

Father went still, a hard glint in his eyes that caused me to sink low in my chair. His voice was almost conversational. "It's funny you say that, Dani. A few of the boys mentioned they'd seen you around the docks recently, dressed all fine." His gaze pierced hers. "I know you Dani; I know you hate it down there. What was so important that you'd risk the smell and the filth?"

My heart pounded. I knew what she'd been doing. So did Logan.

We'd been playing a game, following a cat we'd glimpsed on the coastal hills behind the village. We'd watched it creep into town; the bones visible beneath its dirty, white fur. Skittish and feral, it would hiss and scamper away if we came close. It was a challenge a five-year-old couldn't resist.

We maintained our distance as we tracked it to the docks, knowing it sought a meal of the fish guts that permeated the air. We saw it slip into one of the warehouses.

"Come on; we can trap it!" I urged Logan.

"What if we get caught?" he whispered.

I reached out and gripped his hand. "No one will catch us," I said confidently.

We slunk into the building and crouched behind a pallet of drums, searching for the cat. It was the sounds that alerted us— grunting, moaning, then a rhythmic slapping. I froze, a finger to my lips as I cautiously peered around the pallet.

I saw two figures. One was Mother—unmistakable with her long, dark hair—her dress about her waist. She was entangled in a tight embrace with a tall, bearded man. He was wearing fancy black shoes, clean and shiny. There was only one family with shoes like that in our village.

A cold tendril of dread stirred in my stomach. I knew what she was doing was wrong. My first thought was to check if Logan had seen. He had. His distress triggered that tingle on the back of my neck that was becoming familiar. From early on, I'd known not to provoke it.

I jerked my thumb over my shoulder, indicating that we retreat.

Logan paused. "What about the cat?" he whispered, his face showing his reluctance.

"We'll find her tomorrow. I promise."

He looked at me, trusting that I'd keep my word. "Okay."

We scampered out of there as quickly as we could.

Now, as my father questioned my mother, that memory and the accompanying riot of emotions returned. I looked at Mother, intent on her answer to Father's question.

"Lies!" she cried. "You know I'm minding the boys during the day."

Father looked at us. Logan's head was bowed, but I looked him in the eye.

"Is that true, Gage?"

"She's lying," I said firmly. "I saw her with the Provost's son in a warehouse on the docks."

I heard Mother's sharp inhale.

Father's voice was deadly quiet. "What were they doing, son?"

"You know what a trouble-maker Gage is," Mother interjected desperately. "He's just saying that to cause trouble!" She pointed to Logan. "Not like his brother."

Father paused, his gaze turning to Logan. "Look at me, boy."

Logan reluctantly lifted his head.

"You two are inseparable. If your brother saw, I know you would have too. Is what Gage said true?"

Logan looked at me, and I saw the conflict in his gaze. His voice was small. "No."

In that moment, I lost everything.

I felt shocked at my brother's betrayal. Then came anger. Instead of a familiar simmer, it was a firestorm. The back of my neck felt like a thousand needles piercing my skin. I sensed I was on the verge of an eruption.

I desperately looked for an escape. That's when I saw the candle on the table. The flame was bright and pure. As I stared at it, the flame evolved, became a bird. No, not just any bird I realized, a bird of fire—a Phoenix.

Understanding hit me. The Phoenix was a bird of rebirth and fire cleansed, made everything anew.

I exhaled, and the flame burst into a shower of sparks that grew into a roaring inferno, greedily licking the roof of our small fishing hut. Logan screamed as Mother and Father cried out. But I stared at it, captured by its brilliance.

I didn't see the fear glinting in my brother's eyes, or Mother leave in a panicked rush. I didn't feel Father grab my shirt and drag me outside.

I was thrown to the ground next to Logan. Father dropped to his knees beside us, coughing uncontrollably. It was the cold night air that broke my trance. I jumped to my feet, wanting to return, but a hand on my arm stopped me.

"No, Gage!"

I turned to Logan, remembering his betrayal. "Don't touch me!"

Soot stood out in stark relief on his ashen face. "I was trying to save us," he whispered over Father's coughing. "If I told the truth, Father would attack the Provosts son! The Provost would make our lives a misery. It's better this way!"

I stared at him, emotions roiling. "No, it's not!" I cried, pointing at the burning hut. "We've lost everything! I did this Logan—and all because you made the wrong choice."

Twin holes of despair stared back at me, but he didn't have time to reply as the villagers came running.

Reuben arrived the next day. I'd known he was family the moment I laid eyes on him. He'd come to take me away. I was destined for other things, he said, and my place was with him.

Father didn't argue. "Take him," he returned, his voice devoid of emotion.

But Reuben was angry, and he left with a warning. "You should have been watching him, Steven. If you had, I could have prevented what happened." He glanced at Logan, who lingered a few feet away. "You have one son left, Steven. He needs you. If you don't lose the poison—and I don't just mean the drink— you'll lose him too."

Father's gaze traveled past Rueben to rest on my own. His eyes were bloodshot, his face expressionless. I didn't see regret there—I saw nothing, before he turned his back and walked away.

I blinked, resurfacing from the memory; the remembered pain a wound that never healed.

It was pitch black outside as I peered through the window. We were driving through the popular tourist town of Aviemore, almost home.

Reuben turned right, keeping the Cairngorm Mountains in our sights. Five minutes later, he took a hard left onto a graveled road. It became narrow and winding, the forest crowding the edge of the tarmac. A 'no-exit' sign flashed in the headlights, but we kept on going.

I hadn't traveled this road for six years, but I could still remember every stage of the journey. On point, Grandfather swung the wheel sharply to the left. I didn't flinch as we drove directly towards the lofty trees, passing through the mirage. At the same time, a familiar pressure squeezed my temples. The protection wards.

We drove around the last bend and there it was. *Mothacail*. The old Gaelic translated to 'Sentinel', and the castle was aptly named given the treasure inside.

I noted the lights were on in the eastern wing.

Reuben came to a stop in front of the steps leading up to the entrance and turned to me. I could just make out his face in the soft sheen of moonlight. "Welcome home, Gage."

They were the first words he'd uttered since we'd left the Institute.

"Thanks for coming to get me."

"There was no question that I wouldn't come."

"Sure, I understand—you need me."

The old man tensed, then ground out, "Nora's waiting." He wrenched the door open and marched up steps.

Why did I say that?

I grabbed my duffle bag and followed him into the castle. As soon as I entered, I felt it. That familiar spark of power. The air fairly thrummed with it. The energy wasn't coming from the building itself, though. It was emanating from the person waiting inside the library.

As I walked down the long hall, memories of my second childhood surfaced. Reuben had broken me in here, taught me to nurture my magic rather than fight it. He'd been relentless, dragging me out of bed at the crack of dawn to run drills and build physical endurance. He'd tested all my weaknesses, eliminated all my tells.

"Magic requires endurance," he'd said. "And sometimes, we simply need pure strength. You must excel in both these areas, Gage. Nora's life depends on it."

During the five years I was here, he'd molded me into a weapon. Someone who could protect as well as kill. I'd relished the violence. More disquieting was the fact that I knew I needed it, almost to the point that I craved it. I often wondered if this was prophecy playing its part, or my innate urges. Regardless, these needs would only benefit the role I would one day play.

When I turned ten, I came of age to complete my Druidic training at the Institute. I hadn't been back since but walking down this hallway felt like it was yesterday.

The library door was ajar, and I could hear Reuben's deep timbre. They both looked up as I walked in.

Nora immediately came forward to clasp my hands. "Gage! It's lovely to have you back."

Nora commanded my respect. Which was good, because one day we'd be working together. The back of my neck prickled as her skin touched mine. "Thank you; I hope I'm not an inconvenience."

I'd forgotten how petite she was now, barely reaching my chin.

"Nonsense! We're family."

Family. Not a word I responded to. I gave her a cool smile and stepped back. "Will I be under house arrest these next few months?"

Her forehead furrowed. "No. Reuben will continue your studies here."

I raised a brow. "Fergus said I shouldn't resume training until I have control. I could hurt the old man."

The backhand blow took me by surprise.

"Shut your mouth!" Reuben grunted. "I'm still stronger than you are."

"Reuben," Nora said warningly, reaching out to grab his arm.

His frame tensed. "Leave it, Nora."

The words were gentle and his actions even more so as he removed her hand. I swallowed as recognition burned. The old man was in love with her.

I couldn't help aggravating him, lifting a hand to rub my cheek. "I should be flattered it took you eleven years to follow in my father's footsteps."

Reuben growled. "Fool! You've become weak and fallen back into old habits! Self-pity has no place in this game."

"No, but control does," I said firmly.

He stepped forward. We were nose to nose, and his words were soft. "I know why you lose control Gage; I've always known."

I jerked back. "You have no idea what you're talking about!"

"Oh? You think I'm not aware of the letter that came two weeks ago? You think your brother would know how to contact you at the Institute?"

My blood chilled as the fragments fell into place. "He sent it here."

"Yes," he affirmed softly. "He wanted to make contact with you."

For a moment, I found it hard to breathe. "Did you initiate that letter?"

Reuben's eyes glinted. "It doesn't matter who initiated the letter! What matters is that you need to resolve things between the two of you. Logan was shipped off to boarding school after the fire. He's been as alone as you have."

I couldn't believe it. The old man had betrayed me— gone behind my back and made contact with Logan. "You think you're my shrink now?"

"Bloody hell, calm down!"

I could feel Nora's grey gaze on mine, pinning me in my place more effectively than any restraint.

"You're a powerful Druid, Gage," Reuben continued. "I've no doubt you'll protect Nora well when the time comes, but if you don't resolve this hurt between you and your brother, you'll never succeed in fulfilling the prophecy. He's just as lost without you, just as incomplete. He needs you as much as you need him."

My stomach roiled. "You know nothing!"

"You know that's not true." His voice was quiet but firm, as if gentling a horse. "If anything, I know you too well. I also know you haven't read this." He pulled a sealed, white envelope out of his back pocket and waved it in the air—the letter Logan had sent to me.

"How did you get that?" I demanded.

He ignored me. "Why haven't you read it, Gage? What are you scared of?"

"ENOUGH!" I was panting from exertion as if I'd run a race. Reuben was too close.

"You're way off the mark, old man! I don't need him! What I need is control of my magic! If you don't help me with that, I'll never return to the Institute. I'll never finish my training. And you know what that means, don't you, old man? It means all this"—I gestured between the three of us —"will be for naught and Nora will die!"

Reuben's face darkened, and I saw the moment all rational thought fled. However, before he could respond, Nora interrupted.

"I think that's enough, Reuben. You've sown the seed."

He gritted his teeth, eyes on mine with a vengeance. I'd finally rattled him; made him feel what I felt. I forced myself to hide the emotional turmoil inside. The old man saw too much as it was.

Nora turned to face me. "Rueben's only got your best interests at heart, Gage. Do you understand?"

I stared at her, my body rigid, but she was demanding I acknowledge that. I jerked my head.

She gave me a cool smile. "Good. Now it's late, and you look tired. I've had your old room made up for you. Get some sleep as Reuben will be commencing your training at first light."

I inclined my head; studiously ignoring Reuben as I left the room.

A month passed in a tentative truce.

Reuben pushed me hard. I was on edge, my control tightly tethered. He watched me closely and saw too much that I couldn't hide.

I spent any free time I had retraining myself to become mindful. The ability to stay mindful was a true indication of druidic power. If you weren't present in the moment, you were unable to block out the distractions. Ultimately, you lost control and consequences could be fatal. Hence, the reason I was on suspension.

During those four weeks, Reuben didn't bring Logan up again. It should have put me at ease. It didn't. It felt as if time was in stasis. As if something was coming—something inevitable.

The feeling evaporated when I entered the dining hall that evening. I'd only taken a few steps into the room before I slammed to a halt.

The eyes that stared back were my own, but less jaded. The hair was dark like mine but clean-cut; the build similar, only leaner. He was unmistakable.

Logan.

Reuben stepped forward in the sudden silence. "I've invited Logan to come and stay with us for a few days."

My heart was racing to a sharp stucco, a myriad of emotions escalating inside. The word rasped from my throat. "Why?"

Logan's voice was quiet. "Because I wanted to see you."

"That's not what you said to me eleven years ago! Have you forgotten I burnt down our home?"

His brows pinched together, a dark slash on his pale face. "No, but that night was as much my fault as it was yours. I should have helped you."

I laughed harshly, and the sound had no mirth in it. "How? You're a Dormant; you have no magic!"

"That's not what I meant," Logan returned quietly. "I should have reached out to Reuben as soon as you started to show signs—done something at least! Instead, I did nothing."

"You were only five!"

Logan's expression was somber. "So were you, Gage."

Suddenly, I felt suffocated. I held my hands up. "I can't do this!"

Logan stepped forward. "Please, Gage—"

I did the only thing I could. I turned my back on him and walked away.

I didn't sleep that night. I couldn't.

My sixth sense had become reattuned to him, as it was when we were kids. I could feel him with every breath, his presence a noose around my neck. We came from a line of powerful Druids dating back more than a thousand years. Even though Logan was born a Dormant, he had a strong sixth sense. As a result, between my druidic powers and Logan's sixth sense, we had a formidable connection. I'd missed it.

I closed my eyes, seeking oblivion, but it just wouldn't come. He felt too close.

As the hours rolled by, I couldn't help testing our connection. I closed my eyes and searched. It appeared in my mind's eye like a gossamer thread. I reached out and touched it. As soon as my fingers connected with the line, I was flooded with a riot of emotions—turmoil, anger, frustration, and sadness.

Recognition hit. This was how he felt!

I snapped back, breaking the connection. *If I could feel*

him, he could feel me. I didn't want that; I had too much to hide.

I wasn't the Gage he remembered from childhood. I was darker, stronger, and more powerful. I'd been trained to do things; unimaginable, horrible, desperate things to prepare myself for the future that lay ahead. A future that was filled only with danger.

I'd long ago learned that losing my brother was the best thing that could have happened. Having a connection to anyone—other than Nora and Rueben—would put them in jeopardy. Losing contact was the only way I could protect him.

When the first fingers of dawn pierced the sky, I was more than ready to start the day. As I bent down to lace up my running shoes, I tentatively tapped into our shared line. It was the second time I'd made contact with Logan. To my surprise, I felt him on the move, somewhere outside.

I frowned, leaning back. Then I heard a car door slam and the quiet hum of an engine starting. I froze, tapping into our connection again as the vehicle accelerated down the drive. The line was faint, becoming thinner with each passing second.

He was leaving.

The back of my throat burned, and I swallowed hard, acknowledging that his departure was my fault. He'd made himself vulnerable, first by sending me the letter, secondly by coming here. I'd denied him, refusing to make contact. He hadn't left—I'd turned him away.

The rift between us remained unhealed because I'd made it so.

Another three weeks passed in quick succession.

Reuben continued to push me ruthlessly. Every day he found a reason to bring Logan into the conversation, relentlessly reminding me of my loss.

I awoke one morning, again barely having slept. I'd been afflicted by images of the fire, my mother locked tight in a clandestine embrace, and my father's threatening fists. But what lingered at the edge of my consciousness that morning was my brother's face the day Reuben had taken me away.

I shook my head, trying to erase his image as I pushed myself to my feet. Dawn had already touched the horizon, and Reuben would be waiting.

I left the castle, striding across the lawn to the edge of the forest. A figure detached itself from the shadows.

"You look terrible."

I shrugged nonchalantly, maintaining the façade. It was all I had. "How I look doesn't affect my abilities."

"On the surface," Reuben retorted sharply.

"I'm not sure what you mean," I replied in a bored tone.

Reuben placed his hands on his hips. "Stop denying it. Admit it; you're a mess without him. This is the last time I'll say it: make amends before you lose him forever!"

My fists clenched. I didn't want to discuss this again. Time would resolve the issue with Logan, for ignorance conveyed a lack of care. But Rueben was a different story. He wouldn't let me forget; wouldn't stop pushing.

I gritted my teeth. "Just leave it alone, old man!"

"Never."

Damn him!

I searched for the right words to turn him away. Nothing

seemed appropriate. Finally, I did the only thing that would put space between us.

I ran.

I ran like I never had before, my feet pounding heavily into the forest floor. The trees closed around me, their tall limbs standing sentient. I twisted my head back, searching for Reuben but he hadn't followed.

Eventually, I collapsed at the edge of the scrub, the proud snow-covered peak of Ben Nevis glistening in the morning light. My chest burned with more than exhaustion. It hurt.

I groaned. Even though my body was exhausted, I hadn't outrun my internal demons. I knew then I never would.

So, face them, you coward!

I released a breath, admitting the old man was right— had always been right. Without Logan, I wasn't whole. Since the fire and our separation, I'd been missing a vital piece of myself. I'd denied it, knowing that keeping Logan at arm's length was the best way to protect him. The problem was, pushing him away left me vulnerable. So vulnerable that my control over my magic was eroding.

The pieces slipped vehemently into my mind, confirming what my heart already knew—I needed him more than I needed to keep him safe.

There was only one way forward. I had to see him and make amends. My heart squeezed as I made the promise. But fear would not hold me back, although I had everything to lose.

Facing your fear makes you stronger, I told myself as I pushed to my feet. The wan winter sun touched my face in a blaze of warmth as I faced unerringly toward home. I closed my eyes against the bright rays, and it was then that an image of a phoenix burned behind my eyelids. A bloodless smile touched my lips at the significance. *Facing your fear makes you stronger, but so does rising from the ashes.*

ABOUT THE AUTHOR

Corina Douglas lives at the bottom of the world in the paradise of New Zealand. She is a mother to four crazy kids and a wife to a wonderful husband. When she isn't kiddo wrangling and running her various businesses, she can be found doing yoga or with her nose in a good book. After her last child was born, she decided that it was time to follow the dream she'd always had—to write. She writes fantasy based on fairytales, folklore and mythology. Expect kick-butt heroes and an emotionally charged ride.

I hope you enjoyed this short story. If you'd like to read more about Gage, and find out who Nora is and why she is so important, keep an eye out for my debut novel *Daughter of Winter* being released in 2020.

www.corinadouglas.com

Facebook: @corina.douglas.author
Twitter: @CDouglas_author
Instagram: @CDouglas_author
Pinterest: @CDouglas_author

AN NPC'S CHRISTMAS
GameLit

PARIS HANSCH

"WELCOME to the Dusty Dragon Inn, where your every need is met. My name is Diana, how may I help you today?" Diana gave her customers a pleasant smile and a sultry wink as was indicated in her character code, but underneath the counter her fingers tapped the wood impatiently. Who even named places here anyway? Clearly, they all lived on alliteration avenue. A dialogue box opened in front of her—she had gotten quite skilled at reading the text backwards—and her customer hovered over his limited selection.

"Every need, hey?" he said with lewd grin.

With a username like *8packnsingle,* she wasn't particularly surprised this player chose the most popular option. He was a paladin by the looks of it, with a massive golden hammer on his back and decorative, flashy armor. His party was wandering around her inn, the three of them poking at her photos and breaking open her crates. Typical rude adventurers. Luckily, the crates respawned in a few minutes.

Diana's arms automatically crossed under her chest, continuing the scene. If only she could change the dialogue, perhaps it would make this less dull.

The cleric of the group approached, clutching her staff, her amber locks barely covering her elven ears. It was an annoyingly popular race choice, though the graphics had gotten even better since the last update.

"Brian, maybe this one knows about the quest thing." The cleric pointed to the floor where there was the faint outline of an arcane symbol.

The paladin elbowed his companion and she stumbled sideways. "You're not meant to use my real name, *Karen.*"

The cleric rolled her eyes. "Yeah well I'm not calling you eight pack. You've never done a push up in your life."

Diana stood behind the counter, wanting to yawn but she couldn't do anything but smile until they finished the encounter. Unfortunately, she wasn't allowed to intervene in player squabbles, just like every other non-player character. No, she just waited here endlessly for people to come and rent a room they never actually slept in and offload their junk she didn't want to buy. She had more than enough slime essence than she knew what to do with.

The ranger finally stepped in, reaching into his bag. "Do you know anything about this?" He pulled out a brilliant ruby stone with a matching arcane symbol on it.

Diana internally sighed as she feigned shock. It was about to trigger the combat. "Oh no, you can't bring that in—"

The cutscene took over and the magic circle lit up, blinding them momentarily. A dozen imps spawned, their grotesque forms on fire and their smouldering eyes black and beady.

Here we go again. Diana screamed for dramatic effect. It was a fairly low level quest so there was never a day where her inn *didn't* catch on fire. She watched the flames spread across the floor, engulfing her chairs and tables. She had just gotten new ones too.

The adventurers immediately sprang into action, spamming their attacks against the fire imps. Diana shook her head. She'd just about memorized how and where the imps attacked and they weren't very difficult opponents, yet these players were already at half health. They were complete children hiding behind adult figures. If only she could step in and take care of them herself, at least that would be interesting.

When they had finally gotten rid of the imps, the cutscene took over again and Diana acted terrified, pointing towards the mountains where their master, Ildor the Summoner, currently resided. She gave them her usual speech about how he'd been sending his minions down to terrorize the village and hijacked their mines.

"You'll need this." Diana held out the key to the mine's entrance. No one ever questioned why she had the key or knew so much about their attacker, but then again there wasn't a dialogue option for it. Instead of opening up a new mysterious plotline, it was purely because of convenience. It made about the same amount of logical sense as to why monsters like imps had magical weapons and potions stored in them—though she knew that was the doing of Dungeon-Crawlers Inc. Their developers weren't the brightest tools in the shed.

The adventurers immediately took off towards the mountain, leaving her inn in a flaming wreck. Released from the encounter, Diana grabbed her fire extinguisher, hopping over the counter.

"Of course, none of these self-proclaimed heroes ever help clean up the mess they make..." She began coating the flames in white foam. Thankfully, she had invested in her trusty never-ending extinguisher—good for any and all fires. The first few times the code dictated her inn would burn down completely and she'd need to wait an entire day for it to reset, but she wasn't having any of that nonsense. If she was going to be the innkeeper, it was going to be kept well. Smoke stung in her throat as the fire receded, leaving behind an ashen wasteland. Now she needed to mop again.

The world suddenly collapsed around her, her inn fading away into tiny little squares in a matter of seconds. Diana stood in a blindingly white room, a large floating timer appearing in the center. She sighed, resting the fire extinguisher over one shoulder. She had completely forgotten about the system maintenance. That must be why it was quiet today.

Other figures began popping in from all over their world —Jax the bounty hunter from the vampire expansion, Olivia who sailed the Serpent Seas guiding players through a pirate war, even Darius, the King of Oakenshire was wandering around. They all had far more exciting roles than a lowly innkeeper.

"Is The Rift getting an update?" asked Lanie, tapping her on the shoulder.

Diana nodded. "Didn't you read the news? It's that time of year again. Christmas." The players loved it, but it only caused additional problems for her.

Lanie shrugged, putting her hands on her hips. "Nope. You're the only one who pays attention to that stuff, you should have been one of the town librarians." Then she grinned. "I'll probably get a new outfit though!"

"Well, I didn't really get to choose what I am." Diana let her fire extinguisher drop on its side with a thud, sitting on it. The timer indicated it would take a good few hours, but the developers always took longer than they said. "Don't you get tired of your job?"

Lanie shook her head, her giant blonde pigtails bouncing around. "I love meeting new players."

Diana raised her eyebrows. Managing the tutorial had to be the worst role in the game. She did the same thing day in and day out too, but not hundreds of times every day like Lanie.

"But it's all the same." Diana gestured at some of the others wandering about. "Wouldn't you rather be off fighting monsters or going on exciting quests?" Or even getting to explore the world she'd heard so much about from everyone else.

Lanie gave her a hard look. "Diana, we *all* do the same thing every day. If we didn't the players wouldn't have fun, the game would stop running and we'd cease to exist." Her gaze drifted around them. "We're all working together here. It's about finding the little differences that make life interesting."

Lanie clapped her hands together. "For instance, it's always amusing to watch them pick their usernames. Who wouldn't have a giggle at *hearmefart?*" She peered into the distance. "Oh, it's John, I'll see you later!"

Diana nodded, slowly rolling back and forth on her extinguisher. Only Lanie would be amused by those kinds of things. She glanced at the timer again. At least while they were all together she could make the most of it. She got up, wandering through the dense crowd. An unmistakable figure towered over them, his dark aura casting a permanent shadow around him. His cloak bore the same arcane symbol that was burned into her floor. Diana elbowed him.

"Ildor, what's new?"

Ildor turned, his ghoulish face breaking out into a grin. "Di! You've been busy cleaning up after my imps again haven't you?"

Diana aimed her fire extinguisher at him. "Only every day. Can't you send something else?"

"No can do, you know I can only summon fire-based creatures." Ildor lightly tapped her on the head with his staff. "That's odd though. I've been itching to fight adventurers for days now but you haven't sent me any. I thought there might be a glitch in the quest."

Diana frowned. "What do you mean? I've sent at least four parties your way, it's a reasonably popular quest. You want to check with Mae?"

Ildor nodded. "I didn't even see them enter my dungeon so they can't have died." They walked around, scanning the crowd. "You prepared for the update? They always give me that rare weapon drop at Christmas so we'll be busier than usual."

Diana paused, looking away. Christmas meant snow, and snow meant players would be dragging it inside her inn.

"You alright, Di?"

She glanced up. "Just thinking. We couldn't swap places by any chance could we?"

Ildor laughed, resting his arm on her shoulder. "You know it doesn't work like that. Besides, you do a great job, at least you fit the role. I think I'm way too cheerful to be a big bad boss." His eyes lit up. "Oh look, there's Mae!" He ran over, flagging her down.

Diana trudged after him. It was too bad she couldn't at least watch Ildor. It didn't matter if he wasn't suited for the role, the automated encounters would do the work for him. Managing a dungeon and fighting the players *had* to be more interesting than managing an inn. Maybe she could get her hands on one of those elusive scrying orbs.

Mae was shaking her head at Ildor's emphatic gestures. As one of the administrators of the adventurer's guild, Mae had access to a massive database of player information. "No records of quest abandonment. You've still got a few parties in progress, just be patient."

Ildor threw up his hands. "For three days? That doesn't make sense."

"Maybe they haven't logged in," said Diana.

Mae pushed up her glasses, scrunching her face. She did that whenever she was checking her internal records. "Nope, all players have been logged in the entire time." She paused, tilting her head. "In fact, they're still logged in. And they're not the only ones too."

"Impossible." Diana glanced at Ildor. "All players get booted during maintenance. It must be a glitch."

"Must be..." Mae grimaced, rubbing the side of her head. "Well, there's not much else that I can tell you. According to my records, they should still be heading your way."

The timer began blinking red and Ildor patted Diana on the back. "Don't worry about me. The Rift's about to go back online." He smiled. "Take care of yourself, Di."

Diana nodded. People began to disappear from the white room, fading off into little squares. She closed her eyes as she felt herself being pulled back to her inn.

"Damn it." She glanced at herself, spinning in circles. They'd put her in a rather busty red dress with white fluffy edges, complete with a red hat. *Not again.* Diana sighed, slumping over the counter. At least she'd gotten new furniture. Her inn had gotten a makeover too as usual, as had the streets outside. She could only peer out the windows, not even able to walk out the door. Snow blanketed the area and festive lights lined the village. Tacky, but the children outside looked like they were having fun.

There was nothing she could do except go back to her job. Diana put her fire extinguisher back on its rack, patting its metallic side. It was strange that Ildor hadn't gotten any new players yet, the players hadn't been the best but they weren't that bad. Oh well. There wasn't much she could do about it anyway. It would have been nice if they've given her an assistant or two, or at least some patrons she could serve, then she'd always have someone to talk to.

Diana glanced at the photos on the wall. She was present and smiling in most of them, with her arms around people she'd never met. If a player asked her about them, she'd go on a little tangent and talk about experiences she'd never had with people that probably didn't exist. Apparently, Daniel was her father who took her on fishing trips and Didi was her little sister who mysteriously disappeared when she was a toddler. Diana would always shed a fake tear when she mentioned that, but unfortunately they hadn't expanded that into another quest yet. Maybe they were somewhere out in The Rift.

Diana stared at the counter. It was made up of forty-three planks of wood and she could point out every dent and imperfection with her eyes closed. She'd heard Christmas was a time when players spent time with each other, showed how much they cared and even made a Christmas wish. But she was alone. Diana closed her eyes. She wished she could do something interesting, just once.

Clink!

Diana glanced up. A brilliant ruby stone lay in front of her. The quest item? She quickly stood up straight, but the only thing in sight was a white cat. It sat on the counter in front of the stone looking pleased with itself, its fluffy tail waving from side to side. Then it leapt off the counter, saun-tering out the door. Diana scratched her head. The only pets in game were always closely accompanied by a player, and if a player had brought her the item they would have immedi-ately entered the encounter.

Diana poked the stone and it rolled over, revealing the matching arcane symbol. Definitely the quest item.

But that means...

The magic circle lit up, a blinding light filling the room. A tear began forming, clawed hands ripping the tear wider. Diana backed into a corner, her heart thumping in her chest. This wasn't normal at all. A portal could only be opened by players in The Rift and this wasn't a player, an imp, or even a normal looking portal.

Thousands of tiny ones and zeros were moving behind the creature as tar-like ooze spilled out of the tear, spreading across the floor and climbing the walls. The creature ripped a hole large enough for its head, its skin covered in white hot embers. It had no eyes or face, only a massive mouth. The creature roared, pulling on the tear as it began to crawl through.

Diana scrambled for her fire extinguisher, the only thing that was in reach. There were no adventurers to fight it off and her code wouldn't let her flee the inn. The creature broke through the tear and ran towards her. She let loose a foamy blast and it shrieked, shrinking back as smoke and steam burst outwards, its skin peeling off. Diana grinned. Good for any and all fires, including burning creatures.

Her grin dissolved as the creature shook the foam off, lunging at her again. Diana leapt to the side as its claws slashed through her arm and she screamed, a real one this time. It crashed through her counter and through the back wall, chunks of wood and splinters flying everywhere.

She dashed for the door as it flailed in the wreckage, but a red *out of bounds* warning flashed in her vision and she couldn't move any further. Diana stood there, breathing hard. Her arm was oozing the same black tar that the creature was. The embers of its skin were dull and her extinguisher wasn't likely to work again.

Is this it?

She didn't know what happened to people like them who weren't supposed to die, she wasn't programmed to respawn like her crates. She was just an innkeeper. She didn't know any magic or come equipped with any weapons. Even Lanie would have stood a chance.

Diana gripped her extinguisher. Her inn was in shambles. The black ooze was melting through the walls. A photo dropped to the floor in pieces. She grit her teeth. How dare that creature come in here and do something like this to *her inn.*

Diana let out a cry, sprinting at the creature as it crawled out from the rubble. She swung her extinguisher with everything she had, hitting it squarely in the face. It reeled back and she swung again. More of the tar was seeping from its face and the creature seemed stunned.

"This is for ruining my inn!"

She slammed the metal container down into its face. The next second, it exploded into tiny squares with the same pattern of glowing numbers fading off from it. The tear sealed itself like nothing had happened at all. Diana collapsed to the floor, clutching her arm.

What was that thing?

It wasn't one of Ildor's creatures, nor were his creatures coded to attack her. She winced. Her wound was completely black, the ooze slightly bubbling and moving. Diana downed two potions and felt the open skin close up immediately, her energy refreshed. But there were still dark scars. She rubbed her arm. You didn't get scars in The Rift unless you were programmed to have them.

Perhaps it could all be chalked up to a glitch, though this seemed a little more *real* somehow. A glitch was when she got stuck with her arms out and couldn't move for a few minutes, or when her dialogue options went in circles—not when an interdimensional fiery creature tore through the planes and tried to kill her.

Diana leaned against what was left of the counter and chuckled. That really happened. And she had really just beaten it to death with her trusty extinguisher. What a story she could tell the others during the next update.

A real adventure.

Diana smiled. Maybe her job wasn't so bad after all. It might be falling to pieces, but it was still her inn. She waited for what seemed like hours, but her inn didn't reset. Diana shook her head, grabbing out the mop. It was going to need a lot more than a mop, but she could at least try and get rid of the black ooze.

The door opened and several adventurers tumbled inside. The mage took one look around her inn.

"Woah, what happened here?"

Diana paused. There weren't any pre-set dialogue options for a situation like this.

The mage walked straight up to her, chatting to his party. "Is this one broken?"

"Maybe it's part of the quest."

"Don't know, but I ain't sleeping here."

"She's got cool scars."

Diana furrowed her brows. She wasn't being pulled into an automatic exchange. Maybe, just maybe, she could say whatever she wanted. And she knew exactly what she wanted to say. She gave them a friendly nod, spinning her mop around over one shoulder and propping her leg on a turned over chair.

"Welcome to the Dusty Dragon Inn, the best inn in The Rift. I'm Diana the monster slayer, how may I help you today?"

ABOUT THE AUTHOR

Paris Hansch (Homo sapiens) is a fantasy fanatic, biologist and avid reader, native to Australia. Common behaviour includes living in her own nerdy world of sword and sorcery, playing D&D and writing kickass women in fiction.

Armed with her motto of, 'No More Damsels In Distress', she battles to see a world where everyone can stand as equals, have the freedom to be exactly who they are and portray real female characters we can show our daughters and say, 'be like her'.

Will you join her on this journey?
www.parishansch.com/jointhejourney

Facebook: @parishanschauthor
Instagram: @paris.hansch

LOST AMONG SNOWFLAKES

Fantasy

LAURA HAWTHORNE

Edited by
Qat Wanders

THE CITY STINKS. If the humans are aware of it, they sure aren't saying. None of them scrunch up their noses when they pass by the manure, refuse, and other detritus on the street. Sometimes, if I don't pay attention to where I'm walking, I get some on my feet. Then I track it everywhere I go. When I finally find a place of rest, I have to lick it all off with my tongue—regardless of what it is.

I once tried putting a foot in a puddle of water to see if that would work. Shock went through my entire body. I panicked. My first instinct was to run away as far as possible, just to get away from this little bit of water. I jumped back instinctively, as if exposed to electricity. I looked behind me to see who was there. I looked on either side of me to see if I had drawn the attention of anyone who might want to chase me, hit me with a stick, or pick me up. My claws extended out of my paws, ready to scratch someone.

Each glance from each person felt like a spotlight shone down directly over me. I put my belly close to the ground, not wanting anyone to see it. If they didn't see it, they wouldn't know it was there. My back arched up into the air, trying to create the illusion I was bigger than I was. My tail flicked about this way and that.

When people kept passing me with their loud footsteps and strange odors and didn't seem to take much notice. Nothing happened. My muscles untensed. My body started to relax. I began to feel more at ease with myself. I moved away from the puddle, headed back toward one of the safe spaces I knew. I knew of many such safe spaces throughout the city; one wouldn't be enough by itself, for the space could be compromised at any time. Nor did I stay in one place for very long, lest someone come to expect me there.

I walked away from the puddle, my tail straight up in the

air, my butt exposed for all the world to see. I would have to go back and lick it all off like usual. Besides which, the water had been cold, nearly freezing. I didn't want to get bits of ice on my fur. That took a long time to get out. The ground itself was cold, though I didn't notice it. As long as I kept moving, I would be all right.

My eyes drooped a little bit while I walked, the surest sign I would have to take a nap soon. That would mean finding a safe place where I could avoid being disturbed. My eyes went to the underside of a building. There was a space between the ground on the building just wide enough for me to fit through. I could shimmy my way along the ground until I reached the middle. Then I could sleep. If rain did fall while I slept, I wouldn't feel it. I had slept under there before. I could do it again, if I wanted.

Something fell upon my back, soft and light. An ash or a seed blown upon the wind. I looked up to see if there was anything burning. I didn't smell smoke, and I certainly hoped I could avoid encountering a fire of any kind. Fires have a paralyzing effect on me to the point where I can barely move. There's so much motion, so many scents. The landscape changes quickly. Nothing is predictable. My eyes water, and I feel light-headed. The best strategy I had for avoiding any fire would be to never encounter it at all.

I craned my neck up to see the sky. I was surprised to see snow falling. Was it too early in the year for snow? Or just the right time? I had no sense of what day was what—only when I needed to sleep, needed to eat, and needed to seek shelter. At the moment, I thought about doing all three of those things. Snow would mean footprints. Footprints would mean I would be easily tracked. What was more, I would get wet. If the snow kept falling, I would have to re-think what I was going to do next. I would have to seek somewhere warm, someplace with others like myself. They would welcome me back, if only grudgingly. But I would have to bring something. Perhaps a fish if I could manage to steal one.

A fish. I had to find a fish. I could take a bite or two out of it myself—they wouldn't mind. The humans had not yet put away their own food—food they often refused to share with me. I had gotten hit with a broom more than once just for trying to feed myself. If I died, they would complain about the inconvenience of having to clean up after my remains. It was as though they didn't want me anywhere near them—didn't want any animal near them at all.

Just as I was pondering my next course of action, I saw her. Cloaked as she was, wearing heavy clothing, she looked at first glance as though she had adequately prepared for the weather. Sometimes people know in advance—and sometimes, if I'm lucky, I can plan accordingly by the clothes I see others wearing. However, in this case, everyone else wore their normal, somewhat-cold-weather gear. I hadn't seen anyone else prepared for snow. The citizens of the city appeared as taken by surprise by it as I was.

The woman had a slight bulge about her back she was trying to hide. There was something there no other person had. She kept a hood over most of her so I couldn't see her eyes. Yet, somehow, she didn't mind. She could see just fine. Humans were strange like that.

Except...something about her smelled not-quite-human. She walked like a normal human, had the body (mostly) of a normal human. She wore human clothes. When she spoke, which was infrequently, she used human language as well. Not the language I used, which consisted largely of gestures, body movements, and eye contact. As long as I've known humans, I've known them to be as unsubtle as a thunderstorm. They stomp and crash their way through the world, sometimes using their voices to announce their presence, even though none of their own kind is around to hear it. I've often wondered whether they are speaking to beings only they could see. There was no other explicable reason for them to have such one-sided conversations.

This woman was different. She was quiet. Instead of seeking shelter, or food, I decided to follow her. I had to see what she was all about. I kept my distance from her, following far enough away so I could bolt in any direction if she suddenly turned around on me to give chase. The snow started collecting on my back and my nose. I had to blink my eyes every now and then to clear my vision. The ground started to turn white. The snow showed no sign of letting up.

Against my better instincts, I followed her, trying to figure out what was stuck to her back. I must have sensed something in her, or had predicted what would happen. She turned into back alleys—reeking of days-old refuse. The buildings were placed closely together so one person would touch either wall by extending one arm halfway out.

With trepidation, I realized I had no idea where I was. I had been more focused on following the woman than on figuring out where I was. This was a place I would never go to on my own. There was nowhere to hide if something ever went wrong. I briefly considered trying to springboard jump onto the woman's head so I could land onto a window sill. From where I stood, I couldn't tell whether any of them would be open or not. I didn't think they would be, given how cold it was.

The woman produced something from her pocket—an iron key. She turned into the door. I sat down on the cold, wet ground. A shiver passed through my body. The skin nearest my bottom doesn't have fur to protect it. Neverthe-less, I tried to remain as still as possible. I could not afford to draw attention here of all places, not when there was nowhere to go.

Then, the impossible happened. For all my caution, for all my care, for the close attention I had paid toward keeping myself out of sight, the woman turned to look at me. I froze then—not literally. Rather, all the muscles in my body seized up. My mind ceased to function. For a moment, I was no longer aware of the cold, the snow, or even the world around me. Even my heart, which normally went rabbiting along with a continuous thumping sound, no longer seemed to be there at all.

Time as I understood it ceased to exist. The world had been stripped away, sent off somewhere else. Whatever consciousness trapped inside my body now found free reign to explore whatever was outside the world I knew. Her eyes followed me there, tracking me, trailing me. I could not escape them—those blue eyes captivated me so.

Had I been in my right frame of mind, which I grant you is an infrequent occurrence, I would have run away right then and there. If I had, I would have been safe. I would have found food to eat and a place to stay warm during the cold. I would have gone on with my daily life, such as it was, going here, going there, my ears perking up at the slightest noise. That was a normal life—one I knew how to live.

Instead, I was stuck there, a suspended creature, unable to move, speak, or breathe. I could only think and observe. There was something inherently captivating about her—a power welled up from deep within her being—enthralling me. I began to understand why I had followed her. This power had been leaking out of her a drop at a time; she didn't even seem to be aware of it.

The world focused itself back into place. I was back in the alley, staring at the woman as she stared at me, each of us still as can be. Snow collected on head and on my back. I tried to disregard it as much as I could, knowing it wouldn't make much of a difference visually, given how white I was. If I was black all over, I would have been a bit more concerned.

At length, the woman spoke to me. She had a kind voice, a soft voice—a voice made me believe I could trust her. Such an odd feeling when dealing with humans. Most humans are untrustworthy. They all smell the same. Most of them look the same, too. This one...perhaps she was not human after all. Perhaps this is the reason why. I had seen other kinds of two-legs about the city, especially in the merchant district where the rats were commonplace.

She approached me, one heavy step at a time. Her footsteps crunched upon the ground. She knelt down and inspected me, looking me over. My tail swished back and forth, stirring up snow behind me. Her head tilted slightly to one side. She put a single finger to her mouth, humming to herself.

I've said this before, but the behavior of two-leggeds has always been infinitely perplexing. They don't seem to seek shelter from the elements, or food in a timely manner, or companionship. Instead, I see them running about, doing meaningless tasks when they could just as easily be relaxing and enjoying their lives. They build structures out of stone, only to tear them down later. Or they leave what they've built alone, letting it fall to pieces—after they put so much effort into making it. Completely illogical, the whole lot of them.

Finally, she said, "You're not a regular cat, are you?"

I just sat there and stared at her, not sure if I should tell her the truth. I could speak the human language, of course. Not only was this ability not beyond me, it was simple enough I'd call it child's play.

She must have divined something about my true nature, for she persisted, "You can talk to me if you want to."

I paid attention to the snow falling down over her hair. I wasn't worried if I stayed out too long. The possibility of me freezing to death wasn't an option. I couldn't die, as far as it went. This was part of my curse as well.

A rumble came from deep within my throat when she brushed the snow off my back then patted my head a few times. She must have sensed what I was. I could think of no other explanation. Only a non-human two-legged would have been able to determine I was anything other than an ordinary white cat. The fact she knew I could talk, I wanted to talk—more than anything else—so someone could hear me. I had been silent for the majority of my life. I only used my voice when I was completely alone, when I was sure no one could hear—and only then so I could remind myself I did have a voice—I wasn't just an ordinary cat.

Despite having once been human, there were times when my feline instincts got the better of me. Even though my consciousness was trapped in my immortal form, there was still a large part of me that urged me to live and act like a cat. Most often, I let this side of me win, preferring to let my human side remain dormant. Doing this made it easier for me to go unnoticed in the city. I could blend in, act naturally, and didn't have to think too much. I could just live as well as I could manage until I had served my term.

I blurted out, "How can you tell?"

The woman put a hand on the top of my head. Her short fingernails dug into my scalp, reaching the spots my claws could never touch. I tilted my head to the side, my eyes closing. A low purr formed in my throat. I let myself experience the moment—enjoy the attention she was giving me. My claws came in and out of my paws, digging into the snow.

She said, "I don't know. You feel different to me. You've got this...vibration, I suppose. Like there's more to you. I feel it sometimes around people like me. When Souls have been trapped in conjured flesh; they give off a special kind of energy. You probably felt something like this from me, too."

Her hand came off my head. I stood up on all four of my legs. I pushed the corner of my head into her elbow, still purring. I had to think, had to force myself into rational cognition. That wasn't always easy. The cat side of me became especially dominant in certain moments like this one. Physical touch represents community, a sense of belonging—beings caring for one another. A human would not necessarily respond to this positively, for community often brought danger, hardship, hazard. Once animals established with one another they would not cause harm, they understood as a rule togetherness was a benefit.

If I wanted the human side of me to be in the ascendant, I had to cognitively reject the notion all non-violent touching is good touching. I had to reject the idea body warmth is the best warmth to find in a cold environment. Humans did not think that way. I could still remember when I had been human myself. That had been a strange, chaotic time compared to now. Perhaps the most surprising notion I encountered as I stood there was—I enjoyed life as a cat better than life as a human.

Instinctively, I shook the snow off my fur. It fell to the ground in small clumps. I sniffled, trying to avoid the sneeze I felt building up inside me.

The woman said, "Oh, you poor thing. Are you cold? You

can come inside if you want. I don't mind. Though I can't guarantee you'll like the food I have."

She turned away from me, denying me her elbow. She put the key into her door and turned it. The door opened with a metallic, rusty creak. I immediately felt a draft of warm air. I rushed inside as fast as I could, seeking the warmth, seeking a respite from the cold. As soon as I did, the small pink pads on my paws encountered warm wooden boards. A fireplace crackled at the back of a wall. I stood before it, letting water drip off my fur.

The woman followed me in. I turned my head when she closed the door behind her. Even trying to be as human as possible, I could not help reacting to every little noise. I never slept very long, or put too much of my attention in any one particular thing. Being a small creature in a world of large creatures makes one cautious by default.

She took off her cloak, revealing wrappings around her torso and back. She put the cloak up on a hook near the door and then sat down on a nearby bed, moving a purple stuffed animal. She pulled at the wrapping a little bit at a time, revealing a black-and-red mass upon her back.

Once all the wrappings were pulled off, I saw them for what they were: unusual wings that grew out of her shoulder blades. I stared at those wings, larger than I would have thought, so out of place with the rest of her. I saw, too, that her ears were pointed, rather than round. They were more like my ears; except they went outward instead of upward. She had a black tail as well, one that came out from her tailbone.

The woman's pants had been tailored to accommodate the tail so she didn't have to tuck it into them. She wore a white cloth shirt in the shape of a tank top. I might have blushed, had I been I capable of doing so.

She sat down on the edge of the bed, breathing a sigh of relief. She said, "I guess we're going to be stuck here for a while during the storm. I must admit, I've never seen someone like you before."

I shook myself again. More wet snow fell down. I focused on my human side, letting myself channel it, embrace it, making it an active part of me instead of something that was just there in the background. I needed far less of the cat and far more of the human. Even as I asserted my dormant humanity, the posture of my body changed. I took one of my front paws off the ground, wanting to stand up on two legs myself. That would only last so long—until my legs grew tired from the effort.

I replied to her, "I could say the same about you. Not many people look like you. Are you sure you can show yourself to me like this? You're not worried someone else will find out what I know?"

The woman chuckled into the back of her hand. She smiled kindly at me. I wasn't sure how to take her thoughtfulness. In the first place, I had no idea what someone like her was doing in the city—or what she was doing hiding herself instead of showing everyone who and what she really was. The woman seemed like a mystery that would never be solved.

She demurred, "No, I'm not worried. You're a cat. Even if you say something to someone, no one will believe it's you. They'll think it's a demon speaking through you. I've only just moved here but...there's a lot of paranoia in the city."

"I know. It's been a while since I talked to someone like this. Maybe...since the three-legged crow? He comes to see me every three months, just to make sure I haven't sought the aid of an arcanist to seek a cure for my condition. The words feel strange on my tongue. Some of my teeth are sharper than they ought to be for human speech."

"I'm Saria. Saria Brysalor. Who are you?"

"Ikati. That's my name for now. Other people call me other things. Some people assign names to me, as though I have always been nameless. In the crow's language, it just means 'feline.' It's more a title than anything else. I'm not permitted to speak my true name as long as I'm in this form. They have ways of knowing...my mind is not difficult to read for those who have the talent to do so."

The woman gave a hesitant, unsure smile. I wondered then whether she had problems of her own. She had taken great care not to let me see her back. I sauntered about the room, tail in the air, considering her. I got the briefest glimpse of her back before she turned to face me. There were scars there, fresh scars—red, purple, angry, and violent. I recognized the marks of repeated blows by a whip, or some other scourging tool.

Red patches of inflamed skin grew up around the wounds. Some of them had taken on a yellow tinge. The wounds crossed about the middle of her back between her shoulder blades. The palms of her hands were filled with scars from small cuts as well. Her ribcage showed above a flat stomach, suggesting she had been starved for quite some time.

The more I studied her, the more I thought of how much we had in common. I wouldn't have been surprised if she had met the three-legged crow as well, the one with the red amulet about its neck. Maybe she was also suffering under a curse. I could sympathize with her, having served eleven years of my own sentence thus far.

Saria replied, "What's the three-legged bird? I've never heard of this before."

"His name is Samjogo. He's a being of great power. Not demon, or angel, or fairy. He's something else. I don't know what. Just...something else. He's a servant of a greater power, one I don't know much about. He's the person who cursed me."

"What did you do to deserve such a thing?"

I thought about my reply. While there was no reason to tell her the truth, she felt like someone I could trust. Call it...animal instinct, if you like. I told her, "I am...or was, a Fiend Hunter. In my case, Fiend can mean angel or demon. I betrayed my clan, the people who empowered me to do my work. Now they've cursed me to spend ninety-nine years in this form. I have eighty-eight left to go. Then, I don't know what will happen. They didn't tell me. I guess I didn't ask."

Saria reached her hand out. I went over to her as though it was second nature, seeking her fingers with the back of my ears. I let her scratch me for a moment or two before I walked a few steps away from her. I found myself pacing as I usually did to get a sense of the space I was in. Eventually, I would settle down on the ground. If Saria was especially lucky, I would show her my belly.

She mused, "Something similar happened to me. It probably wasn't intended as a curse...but it sure feels like one. My creator would have told me it was a blessing. Even a holiday like this where everyone is supposed to be happy, I can hardly stay out for long before something or other happens. I feel like I have to stay inside all day long. I'm just...I'm in a lot of pain. I don't know what I'm going to do to survive here. I don't know what I can do. I'm not good at anything. It was all I could do to get this place."

I wasn't sure what I could do to help her. I couldn't do anything about my own situation. The most I could hope for was to float along for a while, survive long enough so that

my penance would be served. By then, Saria would probably be dead and gone. The world would be very different
by then, I had no doubt about that.

I told her, "Maybe we can just keep each other company
for a bit. At least while the snow is falling."

Saria said to me, "Sure, I'd like that."

After the snow came, and after it melted once more, the
three-legged bird came to visit. It opened its beak as it
usually did, a question coming out of its throat.

"What have you been doing?"

I saw no reason to tell the bird anything other than the
truth. I hadn't done anything wrong, as far as I knew. I told
the bird about Saria, and about the snow. I remarked upon
the division in my mind between animal and cat, a division
that had always been there. Perhaps the purpose of my
punishment was for me to forget my humanity, to become a
mindless cat acting simply to fulfill my basic needs for the
rest of my life. If so, I hoped I had enough strength in me to
resist for the next nine decades. I wasn't entirely sure I did
have the strength. Giving in was only too easy.

The bird appeared to frown. It produced a harsh, sharp
squawk. Golden light emanated from its body for a moment,
reminding me just how powerful it was. The bird declared,
"She is a succubus. She is a Fiend. You will have no more to
do with her, lest a second curse be placed upon you."

The idea that I wasn't experiencing the worst they could
do to me gave me pause. What more could they do? I strug-
gled to think of something worse than being under the
control of impulses I had no say in. Perhaps, I thought, they
would turn me into one of those birds, doomed to wander
the world so I could coordinate the efforts of Fiend Hunters

everywhere. Who knew how much humanity I would be able to return with another, smaller, animal mind?

I let my ears fall to the sides. I lowered my chin toward the ground and said, "I understand and will obey. Have you any commands for me?"

"No. Be here again in three months' time. That is all."

The bird leapt off from its perch, taking wing, its amulet tinkling. I watched the bird fly off into the sky for a long time, wondering how many such meetings I would be forced to attend until they finally let me roam free as I pleased. I couldn't leave the city, for that would put me too far away from the meeting site. I had to carefully plan my days leading up to the event as well. All of it was an enormous hassle—I would rather have gone without.

I went off my own way, headed out toward somewhere, stretching out my legs. I didn't see an observer perched on a high, distant place. I didn't see the small orange flame he conjured in his hand. I didn't see his red eyes, or the way his body didn't seem quite right. If I had seen that man there, with his wide grin and his sharp incisors protruding from his gums, I would have thought twice about telling the bird everything I knew.

I walked off, unaware. It wasn't until later I would learn the consequences of my decision—and that was when fireworks shot into the air during the day while the city burned during the evening.

On that particular day, however, I headed toward shelter so I could get some sleep. I had to think about where I would go if I wasn't going to see Saria any longer. I needed to establish a new routine. I had grown to like living indoors, especially with a two-legged that cared for me.

The sun crested over the horizon, spilling light into my eyes. I had to squint against it in order to see where I was going. The light was pleasant. I soaked it in, taking my time, walking slowly. A long shadow drew out behind me. A refreshing breeze drifted across my path, carrying with it the scent of lavender, manure, and sulphur. I ignored the smell of sulphur, thinking it was just another product of a large human city.

I wish that I hadn't. I wish that I hadn't.

ABOUT THE AUTHOR

Laura Hawthorne is an author with a passion for demons, witches, gods and goddesses, and the supernatural. She doesn't try to explain why things happen—she just believes they do. Along with her muse she crash lands her imagination to the written page. Laura Hawthorne's books have been published by Spirit Paw Press, LLC.

www.wendyvandepoll.com/spirit-paw-press-books

Facebook: @wendyvandepoll.author
Twitter: @wendyvandepoll
Instagram: @wendyvandepoll.author

THE BLUE PENDANT

Sci Fi Adventure

H.R. HOBBS

Edited by
Spencer Hamilton

"I THINK THIS IS IT."

"Are you sure?"

Chip's skepticism wasn't unwarranted. We were sitting in his car looking at what appeared to be a house that hadn't been lived in for the last century. Okay, not *that* long—but at least for some time. The house had rid itself of paint, either through the elements or neglect, until all that remained were weathered gray boards. The windows were black, as if the house had given up hope and died. The only thing holding it together was the vines of ivy that grew in strips up the sides of the house. But I wasn't going to let the appearance of the house dissuade me from my reason for being here.

"This is the address it gave me when I looked it up, and according to my phone we're in the right spot."

Chip leaned across me and peered through the window at the overgrown trees and hedges.

"I'm not sure we can even get *in* there. The trees have completely taken over the place."

I peered through the window. There had to be a way.

"Hannah, it's like a forest. No, that's not right. It's like a *jungle*. With God-only-knows-what hiding in it. Let's go."

"Chip! No! Please help me find a way in." I ended with my best puppy-dog eyes and pouty lower lip.

He looked at me, rolled his eyes, and huffed out an exasperated "Fine!"

I beamed at him, triumphant.

The car rocked as Chip got out and slammed the door. I understood his reluctance. This had to be my most hairbrained idea yet. Chip had spent the better part of a week trying to talk me out of it, but I wasn't backing down.

Not this time.

Maybe it would help if I explained why my best friend Chip and I were wandering around Acadia looking for and finding a house that, for all appearances, was abandoned.

I'm looking for advice. Not the typical kind you get from your parents or teachers or even best friends. I've had advice from all of them, and it hasn't helped one bit. You see, this is my senior year and next year I'm off to university, I think. And that's my dilemma. I can't decide whether I want to go into creative writing (Dad says that will never pay the bills) or copywriting (which will pay the bills but may also suck the soul from my body). Mom says follow your heart, which is no help at all. Chip says creative writing, which is partly him being a good friend and partly his own bias, what with the fact that we'd both be at the same university.

To add more confusion, I took a survey from the guidance counselor that said I should become a social worker. It appears I have a need to help people. Which shouldn't come as a surprise, to be honest. My strong sense of justice has led me to help several people over the past few years.

So . . . creative writing, copywriting, or social work? And did I mention I needed to have this all decided by the time our winter break was over? Now you can see why I was panicking.

Miss Thomas, my English teacher, also weighed in on the matter. She's encouraged me to pursue creative writing for the last four years. So, with differing views all around, and me unable to make up my mind, I came up with the brilliant idea to visit a psychic, hoping she'd be able to give me some guidance.

I know what you're thinking, but hear me out. This wasn't

your average neighborhood psychic. This was Madame Astraea. The same psychic who read my palm four years ago and predicted the whole battle over proving Ben Carter's innocence when Jacob Robinson tried to frame him for a rash of robberies. Ben was one person I helped, and probably a big influence on social work being added to my list of possibilities.

Anyway, she was totally right about everything and I'm proud to say (spoiler alert) we triumphed in the end. The fact that there were rumors going around town that she was holding séances kind of helped me make up my mind. I figured if she could predict all of that, she might help me decide what to do with my life.

What could it hurt to get one more opinion, right?

"I hate to admit it, but it looks like you were right. I think someone actually *lives* here."

The scowl on Chip's face told me he wasn't happy about it.

Chip stood at a narrow opening in the trees in front of the house. A sliver of light peeked through what I guessed were heavy curtains. To get from where we stood to the house, we were going to have to fight our way through a maze of branches and shrubs so interwoven it looked impossible to get through. I shivered at the dark shadows that stood like sentinels alongside the trees. What could be hiding in there?

"You're still convinced you want to do this?"

Chip's question jolted me out of my thoughts. Now that we were just ten short steps from the door, I hesitated.

"We can turn around and go home," he added. "Besides,

if your parents find out you were coming to a psychic for career guidance, I'm sure they'd flip their lids."

Everything Chip was saying was true, but despite my trepidation, I took one step and then another in the freshly fallen snow, pushing back branches and stepping over roots. I'd been weighing the pros and cons of this decision for so long, I needed someone to help break the deadlock. Another huff from Chip and, I'm sure, an eye roll, but he followed behind me.

I stopped on the small cement pad that was the step and peered into the paned window of the door. A shaft of light fell into what looked like a hallway.

I looked over my shoulder at Chip.

He shrugged. "You might as well get it over with. There's nothing saying this creepy old house is Madame Astraea's, and I'm not leaving you here alone in case it's someone even creepier than her. Not that *anyone's* creepier than her."

"Thanks. That makes me feel so much better."

"I do what I can."

It was my turn to roll my eyes.

I raised my hand and rapped lightly on the window. Nothing happened. I tried again. A little harder this time. There was a sound like the scraping of a chair and then a shadow blocked the light to the hallway. The hallway was so dark, I couldn't tell if the small, hunched-over figure was Madame Astraea or a ghost—until they got closer and the piercing gaze I hadn't forgotten in four years met mine.

"What do you want?"

The stern voice sounded like Madame Astraea, but maybe I was wrong. I remembered a woman who reminded me of a queen, not someone who resembled a crone.

When I didn't immediately reply to the rude question,

she said, "I'm not opening the door until you tell me want you want."

When she put it like that, I knew I better spit out an answer before she disappeared down the dark hallway. "We're looking for a psychic who calls herself Madame Astraea. According to Google, she lives here."

She frowned. "I don't know who this Google person is, but they have no right giving out my address."

"So—we're in the right place?"

"I didn't say that. What do you want with Madame Astraea?"

My heart sunk at her words. Maybe Google was wrong. Stranger things have happened.

In a last-ditch attempt to see if it was her, I said, "I was hoping to get a reading. You helped me once, and I'm hoping you could help me again. I'm trying to decide what I should do after high school, and I thought you could tell me. Or at least give me some guidance."

She considered my reply, and just when I thought she would leave me standing on the step, a lock clicked and the door opened.

"What makes you think I have any answers for you?" she said through the crack of the door.

"It's you then? We've got the right place?"

"You haven't answered my question."

Neither have you.

"Um . . . right. You read my palm four years ago at the fair, and everything you told me turned out to be true."

She harrumphed. "Of course it did." She eyed Chip and me. "Well, you seem harmless enough, and since you're here you might as well come in. Leave your boots on the mat and hang your coats on the hooks."

The door opened to let us in. We squeezed through and both of us stood on the stamp-sized mat in the entrance.

"Thank you," I said, using my best manners. I didn't want to give her any reason to kick us out now.

She waved her hand and went into the only room with a light burning.

"I was just about to have a cup of tea. You might as well join me. And then you can tell me what it is you want."

She pointed to a cloth-covered table which I didn't think was big enough for three people to sit and have tea at. She didn't wait for us to sit down, but set two more tea cups next to the one on the counter. From a tin cannister on the counter she added a teaspoonful of something to the teapot.

Chip and I exchanged worried glances. She wouldn't try to poison us for knocking on her door, would she? For some strange reason, I felt like we were Hansel and Gretel and this was the witch who lived in the wood.

The whistle of the kettle brought me back to the present. The woman—she still hadn't said if she was Madame Astraea or not—poured the water into the teapot and set it on the table. She shuffled back to the counter for the cups and sugar. Chip and I positioned the items she brought to the table so that nothing accidently hit the floor.

We waited silently while she poured the tea and added sugar. I sensed she wasn't going to tell us anything until she was good and ready, so I waited patiently for her to start the conversation.

She slowly lowered herself to the chair. Before taking a sip, she raised her eyebrows in question. Taking her cue, Chip and I picked ours up. Was there tea leaves floating in my cup? Not wanting to offend her, I took a cautious sip, trying to avoid the black bits swirling on top of the water.

"Now, let's get to the business at hand," she said, placing

her cup back on the table. "Tell me more about this reading you claim I gave you."

Obviously, we still hadn't convinced her that we were here for the reason we said we were. If it took me telling the story again, I'd do that.

"It was at the state fair, here in Acadia. You had a booth, and you were reading palms. You told me I'd fought a number of battles, which was true, and that I had many more to fight. That summer we proved the innocence of a homeless man who was being framed for several robberies in town."

"Ah . . . I remember you now. You came despite the reservations of your friends." She gave Chip a pointed look. Chip choked on his tea. "And now you think I can help you make this important decision."

"That was the idea—"

"It's been quite a while since I've done a reading. Other things take up most of my time."

Maybe there was more money in séances than in palm reading. Other than that, what would an obviously elderly woman have to do? It didn't appear like she had another job, although I'd only seen the kitchen. Maybe the whole Hansel-and-Gretel thing wasn't too far off.

As if Chip could read my mind, his eyes got even bigger and he pushed his chair away.

Madame Astraea chuckled. "Still with your reservations, I see."

"Hannah . . ."

I knew that tone. He was trying to warn me that this wasn't a good idea. Before I could tell him that we'd come too far to turn back now, Madame Astraea said, "Don't run off. I didn't say I wouldn't do it, just that I hadn't done it for some time."

The two of us remained perched on the edge of our chairs, ready to bolt the minute things started to turn creepy. Or at least *more* creepy.

"Finish your tea and I'll take you into my reading room."

Chip picked up his cup and gulped down the rest, which by his expression was hotter than he'd thought.

"No need to rush, boy. Everything happens in its own time."

Red creeped up Chip's face.

I took a sip of tea. It became apparent the reading wasn't going to happen until Madame Astraea had finished her tea. Chip and I sat patiently until she finally set her cup down.

"Before we do the reading, I'd like to read your tea leaves."

"Our what?" Chip asked, confused.

"Hand me your cup," she demanded without answering his question. She studied the leaves in the bottom of the cup. "Your leaves are scattered around your cup. This is usually a sign that the person likes to meddle in the business of others."

"Meddling? I don't meddle," Chip replied indignantly, crossing his arms over his chest.

She placed his cup back on the saucer. "I only say what the leaves tell me." She motioned for my cup. "Let's see what yours say." She peered into the cup. "I can see why you two are drawn together. See this"—she pointed to a blob of leaves in the cup—"yours are shaped like a hand." I looked in the cup. "You will always be there to clean up your foolish friend's mistakes."

Chip and I sat dumbfounded. Madame Astraea stood.

"Come with me."

We left the remains of our tea on the table and followed her down the hall. When she disappeared into a dark doorway, I hesitated. A red light appeared in the center, revealing the interior. A large table with six chairs sat in the center covered with a red silk tablecloth. The shelves that lined the walls at each end held books, crystals, and—wait . . . was that a voodoo doll? The flickering candlelight glinted off jars. I couldn't make out the contents, but it reminded me of a biology classroom. I looked to my right and saw a skull—I wasn't sure of what—hanging on the wall by my head. The calming effect of the tea was gone, and apprehension took its place.

Madame Astraea stood in front of one shelf lifting objects and murmuring to herself. Chip and I stood awkwardly in the doorway, not sure if we should enter or not. When she finished, she turned and sat at the head of the table.

"I can't do a reading if you're standing away over there. Hannah, you sit on my left and Chip, you sit on my right."

We sat where she had directed and waited for further instructions.

Immediately Madame Astraea popped up from her chair.

"I forgot something. Stay where you are until I get back."

With that, she hurried out of the room.

Now that she was gone, I studied the items on the shelves. Yep, that *was* a voodoo doll. A figurine holding leaves and swigs also sat on the shelves. Sitting closer to the shelves, I could make out a jar of spiders and the skeleton of what looked to be a bat.

What would Madame Astraea need this stuff for?

Out of the corner of my eye, I saw Chip get up and go to a pedestal in the corner.

"What are you doing?" I hissed. "She told us to stay put."

"I just want to check out this book. It looks really old."
He ran his fingers over the cover.

"Sit down. If she catches you looking through her stuff,
my reading isn't going to happen."

He didn't acknowledge me as he bent closer to look at
the cover.

I glanced at the doorway and strained my ears to hear
Madame Astraea's footsteps.

"Chip—"

"Hannah, come and look at this. Do these look like
hieroglyphs to you?'

"I'm not getting out of this chair."

Ignoring my plea, he replied, "Remember when we
studied Egypt in ninth grade? Isn't this the eye of Ra?"

I didn't answer. Two could play this game.

It was then that I noticed the statue of a cat sitting in the
center of one shelf. Black except for its bright gold eyes, it
blended into the darkness of the room. The eyes seemed to
be staring straight at me. How had I missed it before?

The creak of leather brought me back to Chip, who was
opening the cover of the book.

"Wow! This book must be ancient. It's written on . . .
what did they call that paper?"

"Papyrus," I answered anxiously, expecting Madame
Astraea to walk through the doorway at any moment.

"Yeah, that's it." A page turned. "Let's see if any of the
symbols we learned are in here. I wish I'd paid more attention in history class." Another page turned, and I shifted
nervously in my chair. "I wonder why this page is
marked . . . ?" Chip slid his finger along the bookmark and
opened to a page in the middle of the book.

Madame Astraea would be here any minute. Then,
feeling as though someone was looking at me, I noticed the

eyes of the cat seemed . . . different. Were they glowing this whole time?

"I know this one!" The excitement in Chip's voice ratcheted my fear. "It's a scarab. Remember those beetles they found in the coffins of mummies?"

I couldn't have answered Chip in that moment if I wanted to, because at his mention of the scarab, a pendant that I hadn't noticed hanging around the cat's neck began to glow blue.

"Chip . . ."

He didn't answer.

"Chip!"

"Yeah?" he said absently, studying the page.

"Look at that cat."

He looked up from the book and frowned. "What cat?"

"The one on the shelf that's staring at me."

Chip followed my gaze. "It's just an ornament of some kind. You know how old ladies love ornaments. And cats, for that matter."

Unable to tear my gaze from the cat, I said, "This is no ordinary cat. Its eyes and that pendant around its neck just started glowing a second ago."

"Maybe it's a little lightbulb in there, like a night-light."

"I think it's watching me. Well, now *you*."

"This is really strange . . ." Chip had dismissed the cat and was back to reading the book. "It almost looks like a telescope, or a . . . spyglass?" He looked at me, frowning. "We didn't study anything about Egyptians having spyglasses, did we?"

"Nope."

He bent to the book again. "Weird."

Okay, there was no way that Madame Astraea wasn't going to be coming through the door any second. I was getting a headache from straining to hear any sounds of her approaching.

"I don't know if I have this translated right, but this looks like the word for their god Aten."

The cat's eyes glowed brighter, along with the pendant.

"Chip, you need to sit down. Something is not right here."

"One second. I think I've got this figured out."

"Don't read any more," I warned.

My eyes glued to the cat on the shelf, afraid of what it would do next. By now my hands were sweating, and I felt like I was at the beach on a hundred-degree day. The hair on my arms stood up and a voice in my head told to me stand. As if hypnotized, I walked over to the shelf.

"Prophecy! At least I think that's it. 'Prophecy of Aten.' Have you ever heard of it?"

I didn't answer.

"Hannah, the Prophecy of Aten. Have you heard of it?"

Reaching out, I lifted the pendant from around the cat's neck and placed it around my own. I could hear Chip muttering, but it sounded as if he were getting farther and farther away. As the pendant touched my skin, I watched in horror as the statue blurred and leaped into the air.

Madame Astraea was the least of our problems.

The cat was now a man.

"It doesn't matter if she has or not. *I* most certainly have."

The ominous voice came from my right, and any answer that had been on my lips was gone. In its place was a tall bald man dressed in blue, flowing robes. His piercing black eyes focused on Chip.

"Thank you."

He lifted the pendant from my neck.

"I'm sorry, but I'm going to be needing this."

I didn't dare move. Chip appeared to be frozen as well.

At that moment, Madame Astraea finally arrived. She took in the scene in a moment.

"Oh, no! What have you *done*?" she whispered. Fear, not shock, lined her face. Did she know what was going on here?

"Good trick!" Chip chuckled. "You really had me going there for a minute."

I relaxed for a second, hoping Chip was right, that this was an illusion Madame Astraea did for her clients.

At Chip's words, the man's eyes changed from yellow to red. "You think this a trick?" He laughed. "I have finally been set free."

The man smiled, and with a swirl of his robes he was gone. Along with the cat.

"Do people really fall for that?" Chip asked Madame Astraea.

Madame Astraea's face was a stark white. Afraid she would faint, I got up and helped her to the chair she'd sat in previously.

"Can I get you a glass of water?" I asked.

"No. Water will not help us now."

"What do you mean?"

She looked at Chip and then at me, horrified.

"The world is about to end."

"What are you talking about?"

"I'm the guardian of Bastet . . . The Book of Amr and that statue have been in my possession for many years. I was charged with making sure Ammon was never set free. That's why I haven't been doing any readings."

Chip came over to the table. "So, you're saying this Ammon guy, he was stuck inside that cat?"

"Yes. And reading from the Book of Amr was the only way to set him free. Now he will continue the path of destruction he started centuries ago." She put her head in her hands.

Seeing the defeat in Madame Astraea's shoulders, I knew that Chip and I were going to have to do something to help her. After all, this was our fault.

"Is there any way to stop him?" I asked. After all, we were the ones who had set him free.

"Only one. Those who free him must be the ones to imprison him again."

"That means . . ."

"I told you we never should have come here." Chip headed for the door.

"It's too late to run away now," Madame Astraea called after him. She turned back to me. "If you don't stop him, you've put all of mankind in jeopardy. You don't have to worry about what you will be doing in the near future. You must make this right."

I suddenly realized the answers I was searching for no longer mattered. Creative writing and social work would have to wait. The tea leaves were right. Chip might meddle where he shouldn't—okay, that was an understatement— but we would have to solve this together. Besides, maybe this adventure could be the story I'd always wanted to write.

Don't they say truth is stranger than fiction?

ABOUT THE AUTHOR

H.R. Hobbs has loved books for as long as she can remember, and it's the reason she became a teacher, and, most recently, a writer. An educator for nearly thirty years, H.R. Hobbs writes realistic fiction and time travel adventures that connect to teens and young adults. A mother to three grown sons and grandmother to three little darlings, she resides with her husband in the small prairie town where she was born and raised. She's the author of The Breaking the Rules Series and *Storms and Scarabs* the first book in the Time Chasers Series. To get all the latest news on her books, join her email list at

www.hrhobbsbooks.com

Facebook: @hrhobbsbooks
Twitter: @hrhobbsbooks
Instagram: @hrhobbsbooks

CANDY GIRL

Horror

REEN JONES

THE FIRST FEW flecks of snow had become more persistent now and Guy was having to keep his windscreen wipers on all the time, but at least the motorway was practically empty. The further north he drove, the heavier the snow got. But this was an adventure! He had only actually met Candy Girl once—he had driven up from London to the north of Scotland to spend some time with her. They had met at the nearest town to her isolated rural home, had lunch at a restaurant she knew and spent the rest of the day driving around the rugged mountainous countryside, opening their hearts to each other. She had told him her real name, Caroline, and he had admitted that Guido Carrera was not what his parents named him, and by the end of the day, their souls felt bound together.

That was six months ago. Since then, they had chatted online every day, sometimes several times. Candy, (he still called her that), had bought another phone, one that her brutish husband knew nothing about, and of course he was too thick and stupid to use the internet. The decision for her to leave him had been easy. She had packed her bag a few weeks ago and hidden it where he would not find it. They had agreed that if that man, (Candy had never used his name), ever beat her again, Guy would drive up to Scotland and collect her and take her back to live with him in London, where she would be free from his cruelty and drunkenness and they would live happily ever after. He was like a medieval knight rescuing the fair maiden from her captivity in a tower. It was quite romantic actually!

He had left the motorway now, so he pulled over, switched on his satnav, and keyed in the postcode Candy had given him. There was still a way to go, and the snowflakes were much bigger and closer together. When he'd left home the snow wasn't even remaining on the ground, but that was six hours ago and 400 miles further south. It was too late to turn back now. Candy might have already told her husband she was leaving, so he had to go through with it.

"At the next junction, turn right," the metallic voice of the satnav eventually told him. "Your destination is a hundred and fifty yards on the left."

The road became a narrow lane, then a narrow track, the snow a pristine white carpet some four inches deep.

"You have reached your destination."

He could just make out a gate leading to a farm. He pulled onto the verge, got out of the car and investigated. Then he texted Candy.

"I am at . . .", he copied the Gaelic name of the farm letter by letter, his fingers quickly turning numb in the cold, before hurrying back to his car. Her reply was almost immediate.

"On my way. 15 mins x. C. Luv u."

It was nearer twenty minutes before she arrived. He hugged her and put her bag into the boot. She was wearing a pink leather jacket and a hand knitted woolly hat that was covered with snow. She took the hat off and shook it before getting into the car.

"Everything OK?" he asked.

"Yes!"

"Did you tell him you were leaving? What did he say?"

"He'd been drinking and went to bed early, so I wrote him a note. He'll find it in the morning. It'll give us longer to get away."

"The police won't look for you unless they think you're in danger," he assured her. "You're not a Missing Person just because you haven't told you husband where you're going."

She snuggled into his shoulder. He turned the key in the ignition. The car spluttered, coughed, shuddered and died.

"It doesn't like the cold!" he laughed. Finally it started and he drove back onto the snow-covered track.

"Is that where you live then?" he asked, as he re-set the satnav for the journey back to London.

"No. I couldn't risk you coming right up to the door, though," Candy said. "He'd have heard the car pull up, and we never have visitors."

He nodded. "Let's get out of here!"

"I know a quicker way back to the motorway, across the mountain," she volunteered. "The roads are a bit rough, but there won't be any traffic out in this snow, not even a tractor."

"OK," he said, "you direct me."

After a sequence of winding lanes, they came out onto what could just about be called a road.

"We'll stop and get a hot drink at the first Services," he said.

"Great!" Candy was still struggling with her seat belt.

Suddenly something small and white flashed across the road in front of him. A rabbit? No, a bloody cat! He didn't intend to brake; it was a subconscious reaction. The car skidded, there was a slight thud and something white flew up into the air. The car left the road, ploughed its way through some bushes and hit a tree. The engine died instantly. It was only when the car started to move again that Guy realised that they were sliding down towards a ravine. The vehicle finally slithered to a halt.

"Candy!"

Candy's face was against the passenger side window. Without her seatbelt, her head had hit the windscreen and bounced off. He had to get her out. If the petrol tank had been damaged, the car could go up in flames!

He didn't remember hitting his head, but he must have done, because it hurt like hell. Carefully he opened his door and eased himself out. He clambered through the under-growth around the back of the car then opened the passenger door to free Candy. She tumbled sideways into his arms. There was blood on her forehead and running down from her nose. He finally got her out, and half carried her, half dragged her to a clear patch of ground. He felt for a pulse but couldn't find one. He held her in his arms, trying to keep her warm, but her lifeless body grew colder and colder, until snowflakes no longer melted when they landed on her face.

"Candy! Candy! Speak to me!"

Her head dropped lifelessly to one side. Then he saw the car start to move again, as it slipped slowly into its final resting place at the bottom of the ravine.

Guy stood by the side of the road; a narrow road where it would be difficult for two vehicles to pass, it was pure and white, completely unsullied by tracks of people or cars. His head hurt and his vision was blurry. One tree became two, and he had to blink before they would become one again. The snow was falling heavily, but he was oblivious of it. He just wasn't sure what he was doing there. He had to find shelter, but there were no houses to be seen, not even a sign-post. But he knew he should keep moving. For no particular reason he turned to his left and started walking. He looked at his watch. It was half past one. Unlikely that any traffic would be along. '*Not even a tractor!*' he thought he remembered a woman's voice say.

He seemed to have been walking forever when he heard a voice from the other side of the road. Somebody was calling. Calling a name. He quickly crossed over and headed in that direction. Then he saw the figure of a man. What was he doing out in this atrocious weather?

"Hey!" he called.

The man obviously heard him, because he turned and started walking towards him.

"Good God, laddie! What are you doing out here?" he asked as he reached where Guy was standing. "Where's your coat, for goodness sake? That jacket's no use to you!" He was a big man, in his forties, perhaps, and he had a strong Scottish accent.

Guy opened his mouth, but words wouldn't come out, his throat just kind of crackled. The man took off his own coat—well-worn but waterproof—and put it round Guy's shoulders. "Come with me, you'll catch your death out here! Let's get you inside."

Minutes later, he was at the man's house, the warmth hit him as he walked through the door. "My name's Jimmy," he said.

"Er—!" but Guy couldn't quite say anything.

"I'd ring an ambulance," Jimmy said, "But the phone lines are down. Come on through, I'll run you a hot shower."

The bathroom was small, as was the rest of the house. Jimmy switched on the shower and held his hand under the water. "That should be OK," he said. "I'll get you a pair of pyjamas. There's a dressing gown on the back of the door. Towel on the radiator. Would you prefer tea or coffee?"

"Coffee, please," he managed to say.

The warmth of the water seemed to bring life back into him, and he took his time in the shower, trying to remember what had happened. Finally he emerged, dressed in Jimmy's pyjamas and dressing gown and carried his wet clothes into the living room.

The room was small but cosy, with a wood-burning fire as well as a radiator.

"Sit down. How are you feeling?" Jimmy asked. "How long were you out there?" He handed Guy a cup of coffee.

"I'm not sure. My brain's a bit fuzzy. And my eyes keep going funny."

"You really ought to be in hospital, or at least have somebody check you over. You've got a nasty cut on your head," Jimmy continued, "but the phone's out." He nodded towards the phone on the table. "It always happens up here. First sign of snow and we're completely cut off. The weight of it brings the lines down. Happens every time."

Guy picked up his jacket and fumbled in the pocket, then stammered, "I seem to have lost my mobile."

"Don't worry about it. You can never get a signal here anyway. You'd need to go up to the road. At least you're safe. It's lucky I found you. You'd have been dead by morning."

Dead?

"How did you find me?" he asked.

"I was looking for the cat. Didn't want him out in this weather! Which reminds me, I'll need to take another look."

He left Guy alone and went to the front door. "Snowy! Snowy!"

Guy heard him fumbling to put his boots on as he went outside. Shortly later he came back in, shaking the snow off himself.

"Dratted animal!" he muttered. "It's my wife's cat. He doesn't really like me, so he won't come in when I call him."

"Where is your wife?"

"Down in Fort William. Her mother's not well, so she's staying with her a few days."

Guy nodded, though he had no idea where that was.

"On holiday, are you? You're obviously not from round here."

"Yes."

"So where are you staying?"

"I can't even remember the name. It was Gaelic. I just walked into a hotel and booked a room." He was surprised how easy it was to lie to this trusting stranger.

"Aye, it's beautiful country around here. We get a lot of visitors in the summer, but not usually at this time of year, though."

"I'm not surprised!" Guy laughed. "But I love the outdoors at any time of the year."

"Well, if you're feeling warmer now," Jimmy said, "I'll show you to the spare room, and we'll see what tomorrow brings. I'm going to take another look for that blinkin' cat."

Something woke him up. His eyes shot open and he froze; his eyes opened wider.

"Where the Hell—?"

He was in a small room, his clothes neatly folded in a pile on a chair near the bed. His wallet lay on top. A picture flashed into his mind, and he saw the car slowly disappearing into the ravine, first sliding, then bouncing until it was out of sight.

Outside it was just getting light and a voice was calling "Snowy! Snow—ee!"

The man was calling his cat. It was a cat that had caused

him to crash the car. The stupid bloody thing. It had just been sitting in the middle of the road, in the middle of a bloody snowstorm, and he and—*Oh my God! Candy!* The horror of what happened was coming back to him. He felt a little sick. Then Jimmy was tapping at the door.

"How are you feeling, laddie?" He came into the room with a cup of coffee which Guy gratefully accepted.

"Much better, thanks, Jimmy," he lied. "I'll get off as soon as I can. Thank you so much for taking me in."

"You're welcome, I'm sure. But you won't be going anywhere today. The roads are impassable—it's been snowing all night."

"Shit! Did you find your cat?"

"I saw him, but he wouldn't come in. Like I said, he's my wife's cat. She rescued him from some kids who were tormenting him when he was a kitten and he really loves her. Follows her everywhere. Somebody must be feeding him, but I don't know where. There's a Youth Hostel about two miles from here, but that's closed in the winter."

"When is your wife coming home?"

"Probably at the weekend she said. She's going to ring me and let me know."

After a heart-damaging breakfast of eggs, bacon and beans, Guy ventured outside. The snow had at least slowed down. It was like walking into a real-life Christmas card, even though it was actually February. He fought back tears as uninvited memories forced their way into his mind. Candy! But what could he have done? She was dead.

Jimmy was trying the phone when he came back inside. "Lines are still down," he said. He switched on the ancient television set that sat in the corner. "Let's get the weather forecast. When the weather clears up a bit I can drop you off where you're staying. Are you travelling on your own or with friends?"

"I came on my own," he said. It was true. What should he do about Candy? He should have reported the accident immediately, but how could he? Would he be in trouble? His mind trawled through all the possibilities.

"Did you hear that? That's just up the road from here!" Jimmy interrupted his reveries.

"What? Sorry, I was miles away!"

"On the news. A farmer out looking for sheep. His dog found a woman lying out in the snow. She's been taken to hospital. Amazing!"

The weather forecast was hopeful. No more snow was expected, but the thaw was now causing flooding.

Guy looked out of the window. "I really need to be moving on," he said.

"Let's take a look, then."

Together the two men walked down to the road. A solitary snow plough was forcing its way through otherwise untouched snow. Jimmy tried the phone as soon as they got back inside, but it was still dead.

The next morning the snow was rapidly disappearing, and Guy ignored his slight hint of a headache and went out for an exploratory walk around the property. When he arrived back, Jimmy was on the phone.

"Yes, this is Mr MacNab. Raigmore Hospital?" he was saying. "What happened?" Guy could not hear what the person was saying on the other end. "And you're sure it's Cassie? Oh, yes, her credit card, I see. OK. The roads look fairly clear, I'll be with you as soon as I can."

Without looking up at Guy, he started another phone call.

"Mrs Campbell? It's Jimmy. How are you?" A short pause. "Really? Oh, well I'm glad to hear that. Er—is Cassie with you?" Another pause. "She's not?"

This was family stuff. Guy walked into the kitchen to let Jimmy speak in private.

A few minutes later Jimmy joined him. "My wife is in hospital. I've got to go to her."

"What's happened to her?"

"They don't know. You remember the woman on the news, the one the farmer's dog found yesterday? Well, the police just rang me, and they think it's her."

"They *think* it's her? I thought she was at her mother's."

"Her mother hasn't seen her. She never arrived." Jimmy was obviously anxious. "She's unconscious. What are your plans? Can I drop you off at your hotel? Did you not write down the name?"

"I only booked in for the one night."

"What about your luggage?"

"I'm—I'm not sure. I only had a backpack. I'm not sure what happened to it. But it doesn't matter—there was nothing valuable."

"How's your head?"

"Not too bad. My vision is still a bit—weird."

"Look, laddie, I really think you should get that looked at. You could have concussion, you know. How about you come with me to the hospital? You can go to A&E and let them check you out, and I'll go and see my wife. If they say you're OK, I'll drop you off at the railway station and you can go home—or wherever you're going next. How does that sound?"

Guy just wanted to get back home, away from the horror of what had recently happened.

"OK."

"I'll just have one last look for that cat before we go."

But the cat was nowhere to be seen.

The short journey to Raigmore Hospital took an hour and a half. The countryside was beautiful, but it had its drawbacks. All right for a visit, but Guy wouldn't want to live there. When they finally arrived, Jimmy announced himself at reception and the receptionist rang through to the ward.

"She'll be on the seventh floor," she said with an unnaturally beaming smile.

"I'll see you later," Guy said.

Jimmy nodded, already heading for the lift.

Guy had no intentions of going to A&E. They would ask too many questions. They would look for his car. And they would find Candy's body. And they would put two and two together when they found her. Instead he headed for the coffee shop.

He ordered an Americano and found a seat by the window. There was nothing he could do to bring Candy back. Admitting what had happened would only make things worse. If only that stupid cat hadn't run out in front of the car! He would go back to London, but first he must thank Jimmy and say goodbye.

He finished his coffee and headed for the seventh floor. MacNab, Jimmy's name was, he remembered. He was directed to a single side ward.

Jimmy had his back to him, bent over the bed where his

wife lay connected to a selection of machines. He turned to face Guy when he opened the door.

"They don't expect her to regain consciousness," he said.

"I'm so sorry," he said. Guy walked across to the bed to join him. Above her bed her name was handwritten, 'Caroline MacNab'. Cassie to her husband. But he knew her as his Candy Girl. Jimmy's eyes were full of tears. Could this be the same violent man Candy was so desperate to escape? Or was it all a lie? Embarrassed, Guy looked away. His eyes lighted on the window, and a large white cat sitting on the outside ledge.

"There's a cat on the window ledge!" he said, changing the subject.

Jimmy turned to look.

"What cat? Where? I can't see any cat," he said. "Don't be daft, man, we're on the seventh floor."

Guy blinked, then rubbed his eyes, but it didn't make the cat go away. Instead, it looked him straight in the eyes then slowly opened its mouth in a silent malignant growl.

ABOUT THE AUTHOR

Reen Jones lives in South West Wales with two cats and an overdraft. She completed a course in Creative Writing a few years ago, and at present concentrates on short stories in the horror/speculative fiction genre, while attempting to reclaim that portion of wilderness which the previous owners of her house called a garden. In her spare time she is working on that fantastically successful novel which will enable her to fulfil her dream of retiring to the dark side of the moon and opening a bar.

THE LEGEND OF THE GLASS STARS

Contemporary Fiction

TASCHE LAINE

ON THE SHORTEST day of the year, the winter solstice, my family and I weathered the worst snowstorm of our lives. We were at Mt. Bachelor in Bend, Oregon, for the holidays. We had rented a cabin at the base of the mountain and had planned to go skiing.

But our first night there, the skies opened up and dumped twenty-two inches of the cool, powdery substance all around us. Trapped inside the cabin, we made the most of our temporary imprisonment. We took turns telling stories late into the night, with nothing but four flashlights for light—one for each of us.

Some stories were silly, some scary, and some had a moral or lesson to be learned. The one thing all the stories had in common? They were all entertaining. Both teachers, my parents infused a love of books in us. They also taught us to have a flair for drama and an active imagination—my parents were the greatest story tellers ever!

Swaddled in piles of pillows, blankets, couch cushions, and sleeping bags, my five-year-old brother, Scotty, and I were toasty warm and cozy as we listened to our parents regale us with their amazing stories. Scotty begged for more, not wanting the special night to end, even as he yawned and fought off sleep.

At thirteen, I, Violet, knew better. I knew the sooner I fell asleep, the sooner I would wake up and get to go outside to play in the freshly fallen snow—for the first time in my life.

We had lived in southern California our whole lives and this was the first time Scotty and I had ever seen snow. Mom and Dad had been to the snow lots of times. They were skiers but had never taken us with them on a ski trip, until now.

I couldn't wait to build my first snowman, make snow angels, and even eat the mysterious frozen water! I wanted to feel the cool deliciousness dissolve on my tongue. I wanted to do everything I'd seen kids do in the movies, and more. I was so excited I barely slept at all.

The next morning, eager to venture out, Scotty and I wolfed down pancakes, brushed our teeth, and raced to get dressed. We bundled up in our new snow gear and opened the front door.

On the other side of the door, a solid white wall-of-snow three-feet high blocked our path. We exchanged a surprised look, then cackled with glee. We remained undeterred.

"Wow!" Scotty exclaimed. "That snow is taller than me!" His large blue eyes opened even larger, if that's possible, as he surveyed the mountain of snow before him.

"That's so cool!" I shouted. "Let's tackle it! Scotty, you dig, and I'll push the snow out of the way so we can tunnel through it."

"Okay, Violet. Do I dig like this?" He punched a tiny hole in the wall-of-snow with his small, mittened-hand. Nothing happened.

"Hmm, that's not gonna work, bud. Let's throw all our weight into it, and maybe try to climb it. Watch me first. Then do what I do," I instructed, determined to get out. I kicked at it, pushed, shoved, dug, tunneled, and climbed up through it like a crazy person. Scotty followed my lead.

Fortunately, the snow was soft and not packed down, which made it easy to maneuver through. And we had fun climbing out to get up on top of the snow.

The beautiful blanket of powder that greeted us, and the way it sparkled in the morning sunlight, will be indelibly imprinted in my memory forever. I had never seen anything that beautiful and pure.

We had snowball fights, built armies of snowmen, made snow angels of every kind and way we could imagine, varying our arms and legs, and ate real snow cones to our hearts' content. We went sledding and tubing and exploring, and even helped Dad shovel out the rental car so he could pick up a few groceries at the nearby market.

I went inside to see what Mom was doing, and, well, I also had to use the bathroom. Getting all that gear off was a pain, but I managed.

I walked into the tiny kitchen. "When do we get to go skiing?" I asked. I was getting a little bored of playing in the snow with a five-year-old. As much fun as it was, I really wanted to ski.

"Tomorrow," Mom said. "Since it snowed so much last night, the ski lifts are closed until they can get the roads plowed and cleared. Aren't you having fun playing with Scotty?"

I rolled my eyes at her. "Of course I'm having fun. Duh. It's the first time I've ever seen snow! But I still want to go skiing."

"Patience, darling. We'll all get to ski—tomorrow."

"Cool! I can't wait." My stomach rumbled. "I'm hungry. What's for lunch?"

"As soon as your father gets home you can help me chop veggies."

"That's okay, I better keep an eye on Scotty. We wouldn't want him to get lost or get into trouble out there, right?"

"We sure wouldn't want that," Mom winked. "You're such a kind and considerate big sister." She ruffled my hair and helped me put my ski parka back on.

"Mom, stop. I can do it myself," I protested.

"I know. You two stay near the cabin. Lunch will be ready soon, okay?"

"Okay," I called out behind me, already on my way back

outside and relieved to get out of vegetable chopping duty. The worst.

Playing in the snow with Scotty had been more fun than I wanted to admit and by nightfall we were famished, ready to collapse from exhaustion. We'd had the best day ever and I didn't want it to end. Dad built a huge bonfire for everyone so we could stargaze and stay outside longer. Oh, and not freeze to death.

We foraged for long sticks to roast hot dogs and marsh-mallows with; the promise of s'mores for dessert. I'd wandered off a few feet away from the others, in search of the perfect skewer, when a pair of vivid green eyes blinked at me. I blinked back with my own matching green eyes and held the stare of the creature in front of me.

Kneeling down to uncover sticks and twigs, I found myself face-to-face—and in a staring contest—with a white cat. Her fur appeared to glow in the firelight. Her luminescent quality and the way she held my gaze intrigued me. I eased off my glove and reached my hand out toward her. I waited patiently for her to come forward. She sniffed the cool air near my hand, then stopped. Neither of us moved—my hand still as a statue, an inch or two from her face.

Eventually, she stood up and nudged my hand with her head. She stood still and allowed me to pet her long, soft and glossy coat of thick fur. She purred.

"You're not even cold. Huh, pretty kitty?" I whispered.

She nuzzled me and rubbed up against my ankles. I scratched her behind the ears and felt around her neck, but she wasn't wearing a collar. I picked her up and she let me carry her back to the fire. I'd forgotten all about my mission to find the perfect stick.

"Whoa, Violet! Is that a *CAT*?" Scotty shouted.

"Shh, you'll scare her," Mom scolded. "Honey, she's gorgeous. Where did you find her?"

"She just appeared right in front of me, like, out of nowhere. And she's not wearing a collar. But I think she must have a home... she's super sweet and tame. She's even purring! And she looks really healthy, not skinny at all. Maybe she got lost in the storm last night?" I guessed.

"Probably," Dad said. He held out a long tree branch and scraped off the pine needles. Then he took out a pocket knife and hacked at the branch, making smaller sticks to turn into skewers. "With all that snow, there was no way we were going to find anything on the ground. I chopped these off a nearby tree. They'll be good enough for our needs." Dad paused and looked at the cat on my lap. "Hey, I bet she's hungry. Who wants to roast an extra weenie for the cat?"

"Can I do it? I want to feed the kitty. That'd be cool!" Scotty jumped up.

Once everyone, including the cat, had been fed, we pulled our chairs up close to each other and sat around the bonfire. My new friend snoozed peacefully on my lap while we gazed up at the star-filled sky in awe and wonder. The dazzling brilliance displayed before us seemed to command reverence as we stared up into the clear, black night of billions of stars.

"Mommy?" Scotty asked. "Are the stars really made up of diamonds, like in "Twinkle, Twinkle Little Star?"

"No, honey. Not really," she answered.

"What are they made of then?" he asked, determined.

"Well, I might know a story about that." Mom looked around the campfire at each one of us, her mischievous eyes dancing in the firelight. She was clearly up to something. "Do you want to hear the legend of the glass stars?"

"Yes! I do! I do!" Scotty's enthusiasm startled the dozing cat on my lap. But she settled down again when my mother's melodic voice began telling her story. I gave the cat a light squeeze and sat forward in my seat, eager for the tale to begin....

"*Many moons ago,* long before people inhabited the earth, there were only animals. Among them, lived an enormous, giant bird. According to the Native American legends in these lands, this giant bird, who resembled an eagle, but was much, much bigger, was called Thunderbird—or Skyamsen, as he is known in some tribes.

"Thunderbird was a Spirit god, and he had a wingspan of twenty-five feet, and talons strong enough to pick up and carry off a whale. It was said that he controlled the weather.

"By flapping his wings, he made thunder and wind. The tears from his eyes made the rain. And from his beak, he shot powerful lightning bolts across the skies.

"The symbol for Thunderbird's lightning bolt is a zigzag, like this." Mom put the point of her skewer into the blaze of the bonfire until it glowed bright red. She pulled it out and drew a large zigzag line in the air with the lit stick. It sort of resembled a sparkler.

"Thunderbird flew back and forth all across the lands, making sure the plants and animals had fresh water whenever they needed it. He filled the lakes and streams with his tears of rain; he formed new rivers and paths with his strong winds.

"When the animals fought each other or provoked Thunderbird, he simply flapped his mighty wings and the deafening thunderclaps rolled out wherever he wanted them to, sending the animals sprinting away in fright. If it was dark, he lit up the sky with his lightning.

"One day, bored with merely controlling the weather, Thunderbird wanted to create something extraordinary. He thought and thought about what he could make. By nightfall, as he observed the sky and the stars all around him, he noticed how tiny they were. They seemed inconsequential and unimpressive to him. Some of the stars were very dim, just faintly shining.

"'Ha. I can do better than that!' he exclaimed to no one in particular. You see, Thunderbird spent most of his days and nights alone. Too busy and important to play with the other animals, Thunderbird had never made any friends.

"Way up in the sky, far from the Earth, it was always nighttime—and the stars were always shining. Thunderbird flew among the stars and found a small smattering of stardust that had been left by a passing supernova. The dust looked just like the grains of sand we see on the beach. He knew that when sand gets hot enough, it turns to glass.

"Suddenly, he had an idea for his extraordinary creation. He gathered up all of his strength, squeezed his eyes shut tight, and concentrated his energy on making his beak as hot as he possibly could. Then he shot a lightning bolt out of his beak at the stardust. Instantly, a giant glass star formed before him.

"The newly formed glass star shone brighter than all the other stars in the galaxy. It had been formed from a fire hotter than molten lava—it was the prettiest and most radiant star in the night sky.

"Thunderbird was very pleased with himself.

"Each night, he searched for more stardust and formed more and more glass stars so he could lovingly spread them out all over the sky for all creation to see. He would have kept on making them for hundreds of thousands of years; they were so beautiful he couldn't help himself.

"But one night, he carelessly kicked a glass star with his massive talon. It broke, shattering into a million pieces and scattering into oblivion. Thunderbird realized that his glass stars were fragile, simply because they were made of glass.

"This saddened him greatly. With a heavy heart, Thunderbird carefully gathered up all of his precious glass stars. Every single star that he had made and spread throughout the galaxy, he retrieved, one-by-one.

"Finally, he clustered them all close together to form a beautiful, giant spiral. This cluster of billions of stars created what we now call the 'Milky Way.' Thunderbird believed that if his delicate stars were all in one place, he could protect them and keep them safe.

"Every now and then, his glass stars drifted away, out of the safe zone. When that happened, they broke, and Thunderbird mourned them. But sometimes, he was fast enough to find and catch them. He brought those stars back to the safety of the giant spiral, where they stayed for hundreds of thousands of years.

"To this day, according to the legend... if you watch the night sky very closely, you can still see Thunderbird tearing through it and clutching a beloved glass star in his mighty talons. He soars through the night to lovingly put the glass star back into the Milky Way... where he can watch over and protect it for eternity."

Mom finished her story with a satisfied smile and looked up at the stars. Following her lead, we all gazed up at the sky to search for Thunderbird.

A minute later I saw a shooting star. "Look, Scotty! I see him! Right there. See?" I pointed at the star, rocketing high over our heads. I turned and gave Mom a sly wink.

"I see him too!" Scotty beamed. "I see Thunderbird carrying a glass star! He's rescuing it so it won't break!" He jumped to his feet and shouted at the sky, "Hello, Thunderbird! I see you!" he waved. "Hello, glass stars! Don't break! Thunderbird will save you!"

In the commotion of Scotty's excitement over seeing his first shooting star (I mean, a daring Thunderbird rescue) the sweet white cat jumped off my lap and scrambled for the trees.

"Oh no! Scotty, you scared the cat away!" I shouted at him.

"I'm sorry, Violet. I didn't mean to." Scotty looked down at his feet, starting to cry.

"It's okay, sweetie. Come here," Mom gestured toward Scotty and he climbed into her lap. "Violet, I'm sure the cat will be fine. She's probably on her way home right now, to a family of her own who love and adore her. She does seem pretty pampered."

"Yeah, you're right. Sorry I yelled at you, buddy." I walked over and hugged Mom and Scotty at the same time.

"It's okay, Violet. You didn't mean to," he said, without an ounce of sarcasm.

We all laughed, and Dad declared it time to put out the fire and go inside.

Over the next two days, we finally got to go skiing. It was harder than I thought it would be. I fell about a hundred times. But luckily, the falls didn't hurt because my landings were cushioned by the soft, fluffy snow.

The day after that, we celebrated Christmas. It was the best Christmas I remember ever having... but not because of the presents.

We were happy then. We had each other and we were all together—a family.

Mom's story of the legend of the glass stars stayed with me. And sometimes, if I let myself, I gaze up into a clear, starry night and see Thunderbird rocketing through the sky on another daring rescue mission... with a beautiful glass star gently clutched in his mighty talons, headed back to the safety of the Milky Way.

ABOUT THE AUTHOR

Tasche Laine, award-winning and best-selling novelist of *Closure* and *Chameleon*, loves raindrops on roses and whiskers on kittens. Oh, we're not doing favorite things? Got it. When not visiting her college student daughter in southern California, teaching, editing, or trying to stay warm and dry in the Pacific Northwest, you can find Tasche working on her soon-to-be-released new series, Glass Stars.

www.taschelaine.com

Facebook: @TascheLaine
Twitter: @Tasches
Instagram: @Tasches
Amazon: @taschelaine

SASHA

Romance

NOLA LI BARR

Edited by
Qat Wanders

Grandma slept beside me while I watched the snow drift past the window. We had just had a lively conversation about rainbows. Usually, this was a joyous time because Christmas was the following week, but she took a turn for the worse two weeks prior. We were on borrowed time and I couldn't bear it. I was spending so much of my time with her that I hadn't even gone skiing. Grandma owned a ski house in Tahoe where she now lived full time. She loved snow. No one knew why because she'd never seen it until she moved to the US in her twenties, but she did. Somehow, it skipped a generation because Mom abhorred snow. She couldn't even stand the sight of it. Luckily, Dad and my older brother Sam liked it, and they'd let me tag along. Grandma would even coach me from time to time. Today, she knew of a group who had racing classes that morning where she wanted me to "go show them how it's done." She had such high faith in me. I couldn't say no.

"Ow! Shi..." I yelled when my shin hit the bedpost. I was halfway into my long johns when Grandma's white cat, Bear, jumped onto my head from the bookshelf. She wouldn't leave me alone. It was like she knew her owner was dying and she wanted comfort.

"Watch your language, young lady!"

Groan. Mom couldn't even let one slip. That was going to leave a bruise. I sure hoped my boots wouldn't hurt it more. Dad promised I would get new boots this year, but I had yet to see them. These hand-me-downs from my brother were uncomfortable, but if Mom had her way, girls wouldn't be skiing in the first place. I'm sure she told Dad not to get me new boots in hopes I'd quit. Well, I'd show them. But boy, was this bruise going to hurt. I kicked the bed leg, cursing it under my breath.

"Sasha, I thought we could... Oh, don't tell me you're

going to go skiing. If you really have to do a sport, why not swimming? You could still go fast."

"Mom..." Why couldn't she knock like my friends' parents?

"You're never going to find a boy like this. And you're still trying to get into Berkeley. Shouldn't you focus on that?"

"Mama, it's okay. I told her she could come with me today. Your mom made her promise too. She needs some fresh air," Dad said, coming down the hallway.

"Baba, you encourage her behavior. And you know Mom is not always lucid. She could be asking her to jump off a cliff, and you two would believe her."

"It's who she is. I'm just going with the flow."

"Yeah, Mom, going with the flow."

I ran out of that room before Mom could say anything else. Grabbed my skis and helmet and hightailed it to the car where I waited for Dad.

"You know you should give your mom a chance," Dad said.

"She's always on my case."

"She worries. You know that."

"She was never this hard on Sam."

"She was. Just differently. You're a girl."

"I know, I'm the burden, and Sam carries on the family name."

"You know that's not what I meant."

The rest of the car ride was silent. I just wanted to ski for the rest of my life.

"I'm going to go to Lakeview. Do you want to come?" asked Dad.

"No, I'm going to just do some warm-up runs on Hot Wheels."

"Okay, I'll meet you at the lodge for lunch."

"See you then, Dad."

Mom had really upset me. I needed to burn off this anger before I went up high looking for this race team. I got to the top of the hill and looked at the path below me. Sure enough, my right boot was hitting me right on my bruise. I willed myself to relax. There was no one else on the slope yet. I tipped my skis and down I went. The snow was perfect. Soft as cotton and fluff everywhere. I was the first one down, and I was flying. All my worries slipped away with every turn down the mountain. I couldn't imagine my life anywhere else.

Crash.

My head pointed down the mountain. One ski had flown off to who knows where. The other was attached to my boot and sticking straight up out of the snow. My bruise was going to be even worse. *Great.* Just what I needed. Adding physical injuries to emotional ones.

"Are you okay?" I heard a detached voice say from above me. I pushed myself off of the snow and stood up, not sure if I was seeing right. There weren't that many Asian skiers, and to have one standing in front of me, and not bad-looking either, was pretty awesome. Maybe Mom would get off my back about meeting boys if she met him.

"Yeah, I'm fine. What happened?"

"I'm sorry, I took a dare to jump off that ledge over there and didn't quite land well. I couldn't stop myself in time before we collided. I found your ski, but I think mine is off on the side," he said, pointing down the hill over the next hump. *He could speak perfect English, too.*

"Well, we better go get it."

"Are you sure you're okay? You took a pretty bad fall."

"I'm doing fine. I'm tougher than I look," I said, trying to hide the grimace from the pain shooting up my leg. I better get those ski boots for Christmas. "Can you ski on one ski?"

"Yeah, but if you could . . ."

"I'm already there." I skied to where his skis were and picked it up, waiting for him to hobble down the mountain to me. While I waited, I took a look at the ski in my hand. Wow. Professional skis.

"Thanks," he said, holding his hand out to me.

I gave him my hand, and we stood there awkwardly, wondering why I had just done that.

"Um, sorry, I'm just really impressed with your skis."

"Oh. Yeah. Dad gave them to me after I won my last competition."

"What do you compete in?"

"Slalom."

"Maybe you could teach me some tricks."

"You compete?"

"No, I only wish."

"Why not?"

"My mom doesn't believe girls should ski."

"Oh, that's so old-school. I have tons of female friends who compete."

"I bet they're all from caucasian families with parents who used to compete or all enjoy skiing."

"Actually, they're from a mix of families. Some are Chinese, Japanese, Korean, or half and half."

"No way!" I must have looked ridiculous because, next thing I knew, he was laughing and trying hard to hide it.

"You seem so surprised."

"I'm the only Chinese or Asian person in my school. I don't know anyone who skis competitively."

"Well, why don't I show you some tricks."

I followed him down the hill and back up for the rest of the day.

"I won!"

"You're a lot better than you think you are."

I blushed from the compliment. Over the last few hours, I had wished the day would never end. I was having so much fun and didn't want to go back to my nagging mom.

"Why don't you come over for dinner tonight?" I asked before I could think about it. I couldn't believe I just invited a boy to my home where my parents and grandma were.

"My parents . . ."

"Right, you have your family to go to. Sorry, I should have known." *Good save, Sasha. Good save.*

"Actually, I was going to say my parents are waiting for me to bring my stuff down. I was supposed to go out with some buddies for some pizza, but I'd rather have a home-cooked meal."

Uh oh.

"Oh, great. Well, let's go then."

When we showed up at home, I took a deep breath before looking for my key. I took my sweet time, dreading what was going to happen on the other side of the door. We were met with the hustle and bustle of my mom and dad in the kitchen.

"I'm home and I brought a guest."

"You brought a guest? Who is it?" Mom asked, coming out of the kitchen wiping her hands on her apron. "A boy!"

I think I blushed so deeply there was no hiding the shame that washed over me.

"Ms. Lee, it's nice to meet you."

"And so polite, too. Come and sit down. I'll bring out some snacks."

"I'm sorry for my mom. She's very traditional and I don't usually bring boys back."

"Oh, that's okay. I understand. My mom's the same way." *He understood.*

"Sasha, who is that?" groaned a voice from the next room.

"That's my grandma. You want to meet her?"

"Yeah, that would be great," he said without an ounce of sarcasm in him.

"Grandma, this is Johnny. I just met him on the slopes."

"Skiing? You know how to ski?"

"Yes, Grandma. I love skiing. You're the one who taught me." She patted my hand in understanding while her head shook back and forth. I tried hard not to cry.

"And who is this?" she rasped before coughing.

"Rest, Grandma."

"I asked you a question."

"This is Johnny. I met him skiing. He competes here."

"Oh, very nice. He looks like a nice Chinese boy. Your mother will be proud. I remember when I met your grandfather."

"Grandma, it's not like that. We just met."

"But you brought him home." *I was caught in a net I couldn't get myself out of. What was I thinking?*

"Excuse me. I'm actually Japanese. My parents are both from Tokyo. But I grew up here."

"Japanese! Alice!" Grandma screamed while she fought for breath. Next thing I knew, Mom and Dad were both rushing in. Johnny and I were pushed against the wall, wondering what was happening. "Alice, Japanese. They're in my room. They've infiltrated. This is no good. Sasha must never see this boy again. You must make him leave. You must. Get him out of my house. No Japanese are ever welcome in my house."

"Mom, what is Grandma—"

"Sasha, take Johnny outside. I'll explain later."

We left while Mom and Dad tried to calm Grandma down. I felt horrible. What was happening? I had never seen Grandma so upset with anyone before. What if I caused her to die right this moment? I looked at Johnny next to me who looked awkward and unsure of himself.

"I'm sorry I've caused such distress." You could see the worry lines forming on his beautiful face. It made me upset that my family had caused this. I felt awful for inviting him over. "I don't know what's going on. Grandma is a bit delirious these days, but she's never been so upset about anyone. I'm so sorry she started yelling at you just because you're Japanese."

"It's okay. I think I should go." He had been slinking to the door as I was speaking, and I knew I had lost him. All the times I had been made fun of because of my race came sweeping in on me, and here was my own grandma yelling at him because of who he is. I was mortified.

"I'll see you later?"

"I'll catch you on the slopes."

"Mom, why was Grandma yelling about the Japanese? Johnny wouldn't hurt anyone. He's American like me."

"Sweetheart, your Grandma knows that. But you know her mind wanders these days. Sometimes she thinks she's living in the past when she was still in Taiwan. She'll bring up family members that you've never met and I haven't seen in a very long time. Your grandma was raised in Taiwan at a time when the Japanese ruled. They were not nice rulers and your grandma does not have fond memories from that time. There is such a deeply embedded hatred in her she can't let go. It's unfortunate you had to bring your friend here when she's like this, and not when she was more lucid."

"I'm so embarrassed."

"If he really likes you, he'll be back."

"Mom, we just met. There's nothing going on." She just patted me on the hand and smiled. I couldn't even say anything before she walked back to Grandma. Not once did she ask me about skiing.

That night, Dr. Brenner came and said Grandma was drained. This last attack had worn out her body, and we should say our goodbyes before it was too late. I stayed up all night with her, keeping her company. She and I watched *Legally Blonde*—something we used to do together. Grandma slept through the whole movie, but I held her hand and laughed at all the right moments. Dad woke me when the sun came up. I had curled myself next to Grandma and could barely crack my tear-dried eyes open. I went down to the village where I got myself a breakfast burrito and sat by the fire pit, wondering what to do next. Johnny will never want to see me again. I can't show my face on the mountain in case I bump into him. Plus, without Grandma cheering me on, there's no point in skiing. Maybe Mom's right. I should just focus on getting into Berkeley. But the memory of Johnny and I skiing together kept coming back. He made me laugh, too.

Grandma was not getting better, and we knew it was time. Mom tried to get me out of bed and was so desperate to get me out of the house that she even told me to go skiing. This was all my fault. I shouldn't have brought Johnny home. I knew better. Now Grandma was pushed to her limit. The thought of making another mistake today glued me to my sheets. But that wasn't going to last long.

"Sasha, there's someone at the door for you," Mom yelled up the stairs.

Who could it be? I hadn't made any friends yet besides Johnny. Sarah and Nora said they weren't coming in till the weekend.

Long brunette hair was what greeted me at the door. A one-piece leopard-print jumpsuit with rainbow goggles that I would do almost anything to get. She seemed to have some Asian to her, but I wasn't sure. It was so subtle.

"Hi, are you Sasha?"

"Yes?"

"Johnny sent me. We were wondering if you would like to come and race with us. I heard you are quite the skier."

"Oh, I don't think—"

"Go. Go." Mom said, coming from behind me, putting all my gear in my hands.

"Since when do you want me to go skiing?"

"Since you came home looking happier. You need friends, Sasha."

I looked at Mom, not believing what I was hearing. This didn't sound like the Mom I knew.

"Just go, Sasha. Have fun."

"Okay . . . let me get dressed. I'm sorry, what's your name?"

"I'm Tanya." I had caught her mid-look as she admired her nails, clearly not interested in what was going on in front of her.

"I'll be right back."

"Sure, take your time."

I got dressed and ran out the door before Mom could change her mind. But not before going in and giving Grandma a kiss on her cheeks. She was hardly breathing. Bear was curled up in her arms and gave me a look like I should have known better.

On the way up, Tanya challenged me to a race. I couldn't say no. This was going to be so much fun. We continued to the very top. I knew I could get to the lodge before her. I could feel it in my bones. I would do Grandma proud.

"You ready?" she asked.

"Ready whenever you are."

And off we went. Boy was she good. Both of us weaving back and forth and even through some trees. Good thing Mom wasn't here. Or Dad, for that matter. He would be livid with me going that fast through the trees. I was focused on Tanya, when the next thing I knew, I was falling—and not in a good way. I know I screamed, heard my skis slide down rocks, and one of them popped off. When I looked up, I was a good three feet from the surface in a crevice. There was no way I was going anywhere by myself. I screamed for help knowing the likelihood of someone hearing me was slim. Yesterday, there was a warning sign about not entering a certain area. Did I miss it? Was this a different path? I screamed for Tanya, but there was only wind. My heart rate was increasing. I tried to control my breathing, but it was so cold. In my haste to dress, I didn't put on my long johns. I figured I'd be moving a lot and *oh* I was so stupid. Someone had to hear me.

What seemed like hours passed. At one point, I thought I heard my name, but it was only for a split second, and I was getting so hungry. Now I knew what Grandma felt like being delusional. Every whisper past my ears sounded like an animal about to come get me. Every bug I saw multiplied into hundreds and had intentions to attack me. I couldn't move my legs, and I was starting to get mad. Tanya should be back by now. She knew I was near her. There's no way this should have taken that long. And I'm pretty sure the sign was there yesterday. How could I miss something so obvious?

"Sasha!"

That was definitely someone calling my name. There was no doubt about it.

"I'm right here!"

I heard crunching and something being dragged. Next thing I knew, there were men in red jackets looking down at me, including Johnny. Oh good, the cavalry came.

"We're here, Sasha. It's going to be okay."

Sure. I'll only be a frozen popsicle, and they'll have to cut off all my fingers and toes.

I saw one guy climb in beside me and watched as one of my skis disappeared over the edge. Next thing I knew, arms were being wrapped around me, and I was being pulled up and out of the hole. They placed me on the stretcher where I looked at the beautiful snow-covered limbs above me. What a way to die. *I'll go with you, Grandma.*

"Young lady, you're lucky to be alive."

"You're telling me."

They skied me down to the lodge where I was quickly covered in multiple blankets and checked every which way. Johnny never left my side. Concern etched all over his beautiful face. *He should really stay away from me. He's going to get early wrinkles if he keeps looking at me that way.*

"What were you doing there?"

"What do you mean? Didn't Tanya tell you?"

"Tanya? She said she saw someone who looked like you at the top, but she doesn't know who you are."

"Tanya, your friend Tanya?"

"Yeah, Tanya, brunette hair, half-Asian." *Half-Asian. That explains my confusion.*

"Tanya came to my house and told me you sent her. That you wanted me to go racing. She challenged me to a race before we got to the lodge. We started together, and I only lost her because I fell into that crevice."

Johnny gave me the most peculiar look as if I wasn't making any sense. I didn't know how better to explain. It was becoming clear to me now that I was warm and safe. *Tanya had set me up.*

We didn't mention the event for the rest of the day. Johnny brought me home, and Mom cried and bundled me up in the living room. Just what I needed. An excuse for her never to let me go skiing ever again. My bruise from yesterday was basically black and blue, and they thought I might have a fracture. They said if my boot had fit better, I might not have been so badly hurt. But rest and keeping it elevated were what was prescribed, so I got to watch a lot of *The Big Bang Theory* for the rest of the night.

Bear came and sat with me. I started petting her when I realized I hadn't seen Grandma.

"Mom, how's Grandma?" There was a silence so strong that I could feel it emanating out of the kitchen. "Mom? Dad?"

"Grandma had to go to the hospital. They moved her this morning."

"Right after I left? Is that why you were pushing me out of the house?"

"I wasn't pushing you," Mom said with shame in her voice. *Good, she felt a bit guilty.* But I immediately regretted that thought. "I didn't want you to see her have to go. We can visit tomorrow, but I know how attached to her you are, and I wanted you to see her after she got settled."

"Mom, you should have told me."

"You just rest, sweetheart."

The day just kept getting worse.

"Since when do you just sit around instead of getting back on your feet to ski again?" Dad asked, sneaking up behind me.

"Since I almost got killed."

"Oh, don't be dramatic. It was just a bad fall. Your skis took most of the force."

"Gee thanks, Dad."

"I'm not going to sugarcoat it and baby you like your mom has been doing. I want you back out there doing what you love. Being happy."

"There's not much to be happy about."

"Sasha, your grandma lived a long life. She's seen more than you ever will if you stay on that couch forever. I see her in you. That's why you two are so connected. You know she would want you back on the mountain."

"I'm going to miss her."

"We all are. But if you're happy then she'll be happy in the afterlife."

"But I hurt her when I brought Johnny over."

"Oh, you know your grandma lives in the past these days. She grew up under Japanese rule. You can't expect her not to have that kind of reaction if she thinks she's actually living in that era."

"How am I supposed to show my face to him again? His friend tried to kill me, too."

"You don't know that. Don't make accusations. But Johnny has called multiple times today. I've told him you're asleep, but he is clearly thinking about you."

"Fine, I'll give him a call back."

"You know your friend tricked me, right?" *Why not just get straight to the point.*

"You don't know that for sure. *But* I wouldn't be surprised. She's been trying to get me to go out with her since we met two years ago, and she is super jealous when I even talk to new girls. I have no idea what to do. And I'm very sorry if she caused all this."

"Likely story."

"It's true. You can ask any of our friends. Brittney's been trying to talk to Tanya. For some reason, she's the only one who she'll confide in. We're hoping she didn't do what we all think she did."

"There was a sign on that slope."

"Yes . . . the ski patrols confirmed a sign was taken out earlier that day. It might have gotten knocked down by a skier and buried in the new snow."

"I highly doubt it."

"Yeah, me too . . . is there anything I can do to make you feel better? I feel horrible that you're stuck here."

"You could find a way to persuade my mom to let me go see Grandma. Mom won't let me off this couch. I've tried everything."

"Sure!"

Well, that was easy. I snuggled back down into the couch, thinking he would fail in his quest, but, not five minutes later, he was by my side again, trying to help me off the sofa.

"What are you doing?"

"We're going to see your grandma."

"What? How did you . . . ?"

"I told them I wanted to set things right with her and have her know I'm a nice Japanese boy. I'm not like my ancestors, and that I would take care of her granddaughter."

"You would take care of me?"

"I'd like to try. At least get you well enough so I can beat you on the slopes."

"I'd like to see you try," I laughed. I could feel my body turn a bright pink under his stare.

The hospital was just as morbid as I thought it would be. Bear sat on my lap. She wouldn't let me out of her sight since Grandma left the house. I had put her in a big back-pack with the top unzipped, hoping I'd be able to sneak her in. Worse case, Dad would wait with her in the car. He dropped Johnny and me off, and I stopped myself right before I entered her room. The smell of decay was so strong without all the surrounding smells of home. This wasn't right. Grandma should have been at home. She should have stayed with us and died surrounded by her family. A frail woman stared back at me from the bed. I swear she had shrunk since I last saw her. There were tubes everywhere. Her fingers gave a little wave beckoning me over. I kneeled next to her, grasping her hand, and cried. I couldn't lose her. Sneaking Bear in ended up being easy, and she curled up in Grandma's arms as soon as I lowered my bag.

"Sasha, who is this?"

"Grandma, this is Johnny. You met him yesterday."

"I did, did I? I would have remembered such a handsome boy. He doesn't look Chinese."

"I'm not Po Po. I'm Japanese American."

"Ah, so an American. Just like my Sasha here."

"You're not mad, Grandma?"

"Mad? Why should I be mad?"

"You were so upset that he was Japanese yesterday that I thought I had done something wrong."

"Oh, Sasha, you have always been so sensitive. You know I'm not that lucid these days. I must have reverted back to when I was a child. Your parents must have explained that to you."

"They did."

"Then why the concern?"

"I don't want to disappoint you."

"The only way you could ever disappoint me is to give up. Remember, Bear is with you. She has promised me she will look after you."

"But how am I going to get back on the mountain? Mom will never allow me, and I don't have any equipment."

"Wait for Christmas."

"You'll be there for Christmas?"

"We'll see, dear. We'll see. Let me talk to this boy of

yours alone for a bit." *Why in the world would she want to talk to him alone?*

"Alone? But Grandma . . ."

"Alone Sasha. Don't worry. I will only say good things about you."

And I was dismissed. I stomped outside and waited. They didn't even know each other. Minute by minute passed by, and I found myself pacing back and forth in front of the door. Right when I paced past for the twentieth time, a laughing Johnny sauntered out.

"Well, your grandma is a very interesting and persuasive lady."

"What did you two talk about?"

"That's between your grandma and me." I could feel my heart rate increasing. When did my grandma become best friends with Johnny? And leave me out?

"Let me take you to dinner," Johnny said, taking my hand. "She's asleep, and I promise, you are still her favorite person in the whole world." Much to my chagrin, that did calm me down, and I followed him out of the hospital.

The next day, I was putting up the final Christmas decorations when I heard knocking on the door. Johnny was outside with some flowers and a big grin on his face.

"Johnny, you don't have to come every single day. I can't go skiing, and it's boring here."

"Well, maybe I like boring. And you're welcome."

"Thank you," I said, blushing. "They're lovely, but why do you look so smug?"

"I took Tanya to meet your grandma."

"You did what?! My grandma does not need someone

like her around. Why would you do something like that? What if it brought her over the edge?"

"Calm down. Your grandma was the one who requested I bring her."

"I'm so confused."

"So was Tanya. It was quite comical. I told her I was taking her to lunch, so she jumped at the chance to go with me. But I had to stop by the hospital to grab something I had left behind yesterday. She was so curious about what it could be because I also told her I had come to the hospital with you. When we walked into your grandma's room, she couldn't escape. I don't know what they talked about. But she came out in a huff, not even looking at me. She took a taxi home, and I drove here."

I was so amazed by the whole story that I didn't know what to say. Grandma just made sure I didn't have to keep looking behind my back, and the boy of my dreams could be mine. I was so thankful for her. I ran into Johnny's arms and hugged him. He laughed wholeheartedly hugging me back.

Christmas day we sat around the tree, sipping hot chocolate with Grandma's picture on the Christmas tree. She was with us in spirit, and I could feel her warmth all around us. It was so good to have the whole family here. Johnny even came over so we could exchange gifts. He said he had conspired with grandma, and I was super curious about what these presents were. When it was my turn, I grabbed grandma's present and tore it open. Tears started welling in my eyes when I saw the beautiful ski boots sitting in my lap. Johnny came in after grabbing something from the front porch, and I knew instantly what it was: New skis! My parents had chipped in for the skis, too, and the warmth I felt in that room could not compare to the love I felt for them all.

I watched Johnny practice for the rest of the winter. And when I healed enough to ski again, I raced him and even beat him a few times. Berkeley was my next goal because I found out that Johnny would be there starting in the fall. I was looking forward to moving to California. I'd show those West Coasters what it was really like to ski.

ABOUT THE AUTHOR

Nola Li Barr loves books so much that she once shipped ten boxes back from Taiwan because she couldn't bear to part with them. As an American Born Chinese (ABC) she's always had one foot in each culture, Chinese and American. Forever a storyteller, Nola finally left the corporate world to write full time and share her whimsical tales.

Sasha is one of many characters to showcase in the series to come. If you'd like to start meeting some of the other characters, check out the first book about Anne and Sebastian in *Forbidden Blossom*.

www.nolalibarr.com

Facebook: @nolalibarrauthor
Twitter: @nolalibarr
Instagram: @nolalibarr
Bookbub: @nola-li-barr

A LOOK INTO THE PAST

IN THE FOURTH month of the Egyptian calendar, the festival of Kaherka was observed on day 12 or 18 through day 30. The New Kingdom is the time period of Ancient Egyptian history this short story and the resulting series, The Lost Pharaoh Chronicles, takes place.

Kaherka is the name of the festival and also the name of the fourth month of the Egyptian calendar. It is the same as Khoiak from the much later Coptic calendar and is roughly equivalent to December in the Julian calendar, although some may argue it more correlates to September or November. The days and months move as the Ancient Egyptian calendar was based on the late annual Nile flooding, which could be delayed a period of up to 80 days, and additionally, their calendar fell short of the lunar calendar which the priests realized at some point much earlier than this short story, and they added five days at the end of every "year" to make up for it. Regardless, the Festival of Kaherka occurred after the annual Nile floods, which left behind a rich deposit. The Festival of Kaherka symbolized the death and rebirth of the god Osiris. Seed was sown in earth mounds in the form of Osiris and watered until germination. On day 30, the Djed Pillar was raised to symbolize the resurrection of Osiris and his triumph over his brother Set, who murdered him, and also, as many assume, to symbolize the start and stability of the yearly cycle of growth and harvest.

During this month, Ancient Egyptian Kings also celebrated their Sed Festival. The god Sed had been replaced by Osiris by the New Kingdom, but it was still referred to as the Sed Festival. The sacred Sed Festival was held only after a

King had ruled 30 years and then every three years after with a few exceptions or extenuating circumstances. The Sed Festival was celebrated to renew the Pharaoh's depleted strength and power from the gods and to celebrate a continued reign. Amenhotep III deviated from the usual ritual in his Sed Festivals and celebrated at his palace, Malkata, rather than at a festival hall inside or next to Amun's temple. He is thought to have sailed on his palace's manmade massive lake with the gods aboard his barge to show he was indeed renewed by them.

This short story takes place during Pharaoh Amenhotep III's second Sed Festival of the three he celebrated, and the subsequent Festival of Kaherka. If you enjoyed this short story and want to find out what happens next with Thutmose, Amenhotep and Nefertiti, check out Lauren's highly rated debut series, The Lost Pharaoh Chronicles. Start with *Book One: Salvation in the Sun*.

KING'S JUBILEE

Historical Fiction

LAUREN LEE
MEREWETHER

A Lost Pharaoh Chronicles Prequel

Edited by
Luis Andres

"Son," Pharaoh Amenhotep III placed one hand on Thutmose's shoulder, "Egypt's Crown Prince." Placing his other hand on the other shoulder, he leaned in close. "One day you shall be celebrating in my stead. At my next Sed Festival, you shall be named Coregent. When the time comes that you stand alone to rule the mighty Egypt, Amun will transfer his power to you as his divinely appointed King."

Thutmose beamed and stood tall under his father's firm grasp.

"I will not fail you, Pharaoh." Though his lips spoke *Pharaoh*, his heart said *Father*. However, there was a certain way he had to speak to this great man who ruled both the Upper and the Lower of their great empire.

I will be the best Pharaoh to ever have lived. When you are no longer here, you will look down from Re and smile at what I will have accomplished. It will all be for you, Father.

His lungs expanded to welcome a full, satisfying breath.

Pharaoh pulled away from his son, and in a grand sweeping motion, lifted his hands from his son's shoulders. "You are the perfect son of Pharaoh. You are mighty and strong and quick with your reason." His hands fell to cup Thutmose's face. "You are wise and will do well in Pharaoh's place. Now observe this time with care, as it will be yours in the coming years."

He scowled as his eyes darted to his second-born son shouting praise in the courtyard to the sun disc, the Aten. Letting out a frustrated sigh, he shook his head. Gripping his son's neck and pulling his forehead to his, he whispered to Thutmose. "Look after your brother for he lacks all that you are." Pharaoh removed his hands from Thutmose's neck and stood erect once again. "Even if you must keep him secluded in my great palace, Malkata."

He gestured for Thutmose to walk with him down the courtyard's open corridor to Malkata's impressive lake.

Thutmose peered over his shoulder to observe his eleven-year-old brother standing out in the sun without so much as a heavy linen wrap around his body despite the unusually cold day. *I don't think I will take care of him. He doesn't even honor our father during this time.* He turned up his nose and walked with a proud chest alongside Pharaoh.

"Thutmose, when you become Pharaoh, you will face a growing threat to your throne. The priesthood of Amun-Re grows in power every day. I have made strides to keep them from overtaking the throne, but Meryptah appointed himself as First Prophet of Amun, an action traditionally reserved for Pharaoh." His father sighed and squinted from the sun's rays sparkling over the lake in the distance. "This is why we do not celebrate my Sed Festival in the temple of Amun. If we did, we would only increase their power over the throne. Pharaoh is the true First Prophet, not some priest. Thus, we celebrate here at Malkata. Pharaohs before have run with the Apis Bull to show their strength and fired their arrows in each of the four directions to show their dominance over the lands. Yet I will sail across Malkata's lake and return symbolizing Osiris' death and resurrection, and it will be known that I have made the same journey. Pharaoh returns to his people renewed with the lifeforce of the gods."

Thutmose nodded his head, soaking in all what his father said. "I understand, Pharaoh." He bit his lip, afraid to ask the questions that raced through his mind.

His father chuckled, but his eyes remained bright as he glanced toward his son. "No, you do not."

Thutmose's chest caved a bit. "I need more time to understand."

"Yes." Pharaoh nodded seemingly pleased with his son's response. "Your mother, my chief royal wife and Queen, Tiye, will help you before my next Sed Festival," Pharaoh said as a relaxed smile crossed his lips. "Then you will be crowned Coregent and you will understand. You shall train as a priest of Ptah in Men-nefer to further draw power away from the priesthood of Amun."

Thutmose's heart sank. He did not want to leave Malkata, but at least it would be a short few years before he was crowned Coregent and could return. "Does Amenhotep know about this threat to the throne?" Thutmose asked as he peered up to his father.

"No, that boy wouldn't understand a rock if it was laid at his feet." He clenched his jaw and shut his eyes. "Your poor brother–"

"He can't even throw a rock." Thutmose smirked remembering the sad attempt his brother made when competing for sports and the way he habitually dropped every weapon with which they trained.

"He was a sickly child," Pharaoh nodded in an attempt to hide his smile at Thutmose's comment. "I always thought he would grow into a man, but his time dwindles, and I have little hope he will ever reach the expectations for a son of Pharaoh."

Thutmose nodded. Amenhotep only had four years left before he was considered old enough to marry, and he would lose his sidelock soon, too. *He might as well be hopeless*, he thought listening to the remnants of his odd worship of the Aten echoing off the stone wall as they walked.

"That is why the gods granted me a perfect firstborn son," Pharaoh wrapped his arm around Thutmose and pulled him into a side embrace. He stopped just short of the shadow's end and turned to Thutmose once more. "I am proud to call you mine."

He dropped his arms, and the royal guards, who had lingered behind them, came forth and escorted Pharaoh forth from the shadow to go onward toward the nobles who had gathered for this last day of his Sed Festival. The commoners watched from the other side of the Nile River. Thutmose found his mother, Queen Tiye, waiting for his father to join her.

Thutmose ran around the courtyard and, out of fun, pushed his brother Amenhotep from his worship before heading to the balcony where their sisters awaited him. He heard his brother curse him and his footsteps behind him, but he went to a full sprint and lost him. After a moment, he stopped and turned around, not even winded. At the end of the corridor, Amenhotep stood hunched over, struggling for breath.

Thutmose laughed and, knowing his voice would carry across the stone, said, "That is why I am Crown Prince and you are not."

His brother's response came back to him. "I never wanted to be Crown Prince. Just let me be."

Thutmose sneered. *Only my foolish brother would not want to rule Egypt. Weak.* "Are you coming to watch Pharaoh?"

"No. Kasmut is coming to–"

"You are a fool," Thutmose said as he walked away.

"No, you are." Amenhotep's voice trailed him.

Thutmose shook off the insult. *No need to waste time on him. Even father doesn't want him depicted as his son on the reliefs and statues in the temples.*

He made his way to the balcony where sat his two eldest sisters, Sitamun and Iset, who were also married to Pharaoh, and his two elder sisters, Nebetah and Henuttaneb, whom his father said would marry him when he became Coregent. The four sisters dipped their head to Thutmose as he took his seat.

"You were almost late, Thutmose," Sitamun chided.

He looked to her. There was an elegance in the way she held herself, her chin perched parallel to the ground at all times and her voice flowed as smooth as the Nile River.

"Crown Prince Thutmose to you," he jested.

"I will call you by your appropriate title when you choose to be on time, my dear brother," Sitamun said and turned to peer at him.

He narrowed his eyes to her. "I am on time, *sister*."

They both looked forward and watched their father address the large mass of nobles and officials. Thutmose found his eyes wandering the crowd, trying to pick out a certain officer's daughter.

"You are to watch father, brother," Iset chimed in, her voice a little higher than Sitamun's.

Thutmose realized he had leaned forward to scan the crowd. He shot her a glare.

"I *am* watching father."

"Nefertiti can wait," Sitamun said. "Tonight is about father. You should watch and listen as you will be by his side at the next Sed Festival."

"I already know what to say and what to do," he sneered and continued to look for Nefertiti.

Henuttaneb tapped his shoulder and pointed. He followed the indication of her finger before she lowered her hand not to make it obvious to any noble who happened to look up at them that they were not watching Pharaoh.

He spotted her. Standing tall, wrapped in a linen cloak, her sidelock shining in the sun's rays, she stood next to her father Ay, Overseer of Pharaoh's Horses and brother to Queen Tiye. He felt his own sidelock against his ear and knew in one more year, it would be removed. His heart raced waiting for that day. For the rest of the Sed Festival his eyes darted between his father and Nefertiti.

Priests began placing the animal representations of the gods onto Pharaoh's barge and, once finished, Pharaoh disembarked to sail across his lake. It was as if the gods wanted the scene to appear surreal, as a light fog arose from the waters and a sudden cold breeze pressed upon the people. Pharaoh disappeared into the fog.

A great murmur swept through the nobles. Was Pharaoh to return from the dead as Osiris once did?

Thutmose saw his sisters wringing their hands and realized his own were clenched into fists, waiting to see if his father succeeded. Then, a hush fell upon the people as they leaned toward the lake, their eyes searching and scanning for any sign of their Pharaoh.

What seemed like a lifetime passed until the tip of the barge struck through the fog, and Pharaoh came sailing through. The people erupted in victory. Thutmose felt his heart well within his chest, proud his father made such a journey. The abundant offerings to the gods had not been in vain for they granted him successful passage.

After the Sed Festival ended and the sun descended to the west, Thutmose found Nefertiti lingering next to Ay. She looked up to her father, who was engrossed in conversation with vizier Huy, and then snuck away to speak with Thutmose. She smiled, and his inhibitions melt away. Her cheeks rose as high as the sun, her lips were as red as the rose, and her eyes as black as kohl.

"Did you enjoy Pharaoh's Sed Festival?" he asked, knowing people could overhear their conversation. It was not the time to sit and share secrets as they had done in the past in a forgotten corridor of Malkata.

"I did, Crown Prince Thutmose," she said and bowed to him. Her eyes danced in the flame of the alabaster torches lining the hall.

"Would you walk with me?" Thutmose asked. She nodded, and he led her away from the people, slipping past his guards until they were out of the hall and into the courtyard.

He felt a rush within him. Not able to contain himself any longer, he kissed her on her cheek. She was silent for a moment, and then they both laughed.

"Crown Prince!" she squealed and put her hand to her cheek as her smile grew from ear to ear.

"Crown Prince," a voice whined and mocked in the dark.

Two figures came up behind her.

Thutmose looked and then dropped his shoulders upon his recognition of them. "What do *you* want brother?"

"What I want is for the Aten to show his face again to heal me of my pain," Amenhotep said pointing to the sky, "but I never get what I want."

"That is why you should want to be Crown Prince. You would always get what you want." Thutmose put his arm around Nefertiti and pulled her close to him.

Kasmut appeared next to Amenhotep.

"Did you, daughter of Anen, not take part in Pharaoh's sacred Sed Festival either?" Thutmose glowered at her.

"Prince Amenhotep needed me by his side," she responded and looked to her cousin, Nefertiti. "Why must you be so harsh, Crown Prince?" her eyes darted back to Thutmose. "Your mother is our fathers' sister. We are all family here."

Thutmose's feet shuffled backward in response to such a blunt question from her. "You dare speak to the Crown Prince in such a manner?"

Nefertiti only looked to the ground.

"Prince Amenhotep is your brother," Kasmut said, looking him in the eye. "He told me what you said to him. He is still a son of Pharaoh–"

"Silence, Kasmut, daughter of Anen," Thutmose's voice dropped, and he thanked the gods it did not crack as it had been doing lately.

"Come on, Kasmut," Amenhotep put his arms around her and pulled her close. "We shall leave the Crown Prince to his selfish ways. He said he could have anything he wanted, but I am glad I am not Crown Prince, for then I can have you." He smiled at Kasmut and then looked to Thutmose.

Thutmose studied his long face and long fingers draping over Kasmut's shoulder. "Be gone, your senses have scattered anyway."

Amenhotep narrowed his eyes at his brother and a scowl grew on his lips at the cruel insult.

Kasmut patted his hand to calm him.

"Don't bother with him," she whispered and led him away.

Thutmose laughed and then, turning back to Nefertiti, said, "He can't even defend himself. He would not make a good Pharaoh. He would be the worst..." his voice trailed off at the sadness in Nefertiti's eyes. "What?"

"He is your brother," she whispered. "He is not as

blessed as you are. The gods have granted you wit, strength, physical prowess, excellence in your studies–"

"Enough," Thutmose averted his eyes as a pink hue graced his cheeks, and he thanked the Aten for not showing his face at night. They stood there in silence for a moment. He did not know what to say, or if he should apologize for his outburst, but his father's words came back to him as they did every time, *Pharaoh does not apologize.*

Nefertiti finally grasped his hand and pulled it close to her chest. "You will be a wise King," she nodded. "I have no doubts in you."

He found her gaze again and felt something lingered on her tongue.

"But..."

Her brow furrowed. "A wise man hears those brave enough to challenge his ways if to better himself," Nefertiti whispered and smiled a half-smile.

He pursed his lips. *A noble's daughter wiser than me?* He pulled his hand away and lifted his chin. "I am no ordinary man. I am the Crown Prince."

"Yes, you are," she snapped and took a step backward. Bowing to him, her voice held a monotonous tone. "Sleep well, Crown Prince." Then, she turned to leave.

He wanted to call out to her, but his stiff neck and weighted chest repressed his desire. Instead, he turned his gaze and stared off into the darkness. Little did he know his mother had been watching him from the hall's edge.

The next day at the start of the Festival of Kaherka, the people formed mounds out of the earth in the form of Osiris and sowed seed in them for their next crop. Thutmose received a message from his mother to meet her in the Malkata temple Pharaoh had built and dedicated to her worship. He found her kneeling before the alabaster image of Bastet, the goddess who took the form of a cat. Without looking up, she said, "Kneel with me, my son."

He knelt sitting back on his heels.

"Do you know why I pray to Bastet?" she whispered.

"She is the goddess of the home, women and children." He shrugged.

"Yes...and of women's secrets." She looked to Bastet's opaque polished alabaster form and stared into her painted black eyes. "I have prayed about my secrets to Bastet for a long time."

His eyes crept over to his mother and saw tears welling in her eyes. "I ask for forgiveness as a mother." She dropped her head and brought her hands to her chest, her whole back bowing to the goddess.

Thutmose bit his lip before placing a hesitant hand on her shoulder. "But Mother, you have done nothing requiring forgiveness."

"Oh, my son, I have," she said finding his gaze. "I heard you in the courtyard."

His ears turned red. "You were spying?"

"No, I happened by." She drew in a long, cleansing breath and stayed her tears for the moment. "Thutmose, what I will tell you, you must promise me you will never tell a soul, on the jeopardy of your afterlife." Her voice wavered, but her eyes stayed firm.

He nodded knowing if he told, the demoness goddess, Ammit, may devour his heart, and he would never have eternal peace.

"After all these years, I have found my husband to be a prideful man, one who threatened to strip me of my title for standing up for my own son. How can I be so proud for the one who has and was given everything including his father's love, and yet for the other son, given nothing, alienated, simply because his father is ashamed he carries his name." Tears fell from her eyes as she glanced back to Bastet. "I stayed silent because I knew I could help Amenhotep more as Queen than if exile befell me, but now," she looked into his eyes again, "I see you acting as your father."

"But Mother," Thutmose rubbed the back of his neck, "Amenhotep is weak, he is not worthy to be a son of Pharaoh."

"He is my son," Queen Tiye's words sliced through the air between them. "As are you."

Thutmose, though Crown Prince, knew that tone meant he should not say any more.

"Bastet has kept watch over my secret, and I tell you now: do not become your father in this regard. If he had given Amenhotep the same love he gave you, do you think Amenhotep would be the same as he is today?"

Thutmose forgot how to breathe in that moment as the question looped in his mind. He could only stare at his mother through wide eyes as a heavy weight grew roots in his stomach.

"I pray to Bastet for you, that you may see your father's folly. He is a mighty Pharaoh. Egypt is the better because of him, but I feel in my heart, he was wrong about your brother." She turned to look back at the white alabaster cat goddess. "You are the Crown Prince. You will rule someday, and I ask you, as your mother, to reconsider your brother."

Father can do no wrong. He is Pharaoh and a great father. He... his mind numbed in refusal to believe his mother, or so he told himself. Thutmose clenched his jaw, not knowing whether to scream at her or his father. So, instead, he stood and left his mother praying to Bastet.

"Ah, there is my son," Pharaoh said as he entered the royal harem with a warm smile on his lips, opening his arms toward Thutmose.

Amenhotep did not notice either one as he twirled in the sun's rays, asking the Aten for healing. Thutmose stood and bowed to his father just as Amenhotep ran into Pharaoh's back on accident.

Pharaoh jerked back pressing his lips into a grimace. "You, ignorant child," Pharaoh turned and pushed Amenhotep away, setting his hard stare upon him. "You dare insult Pharaoh?"

"No," Amenhotep's head dropped along with his shoulders.

"Why can't you be like your brother?!" Pharaoh shoved a hand in Thutmose's direction. "Why do the gods curse me with a son who falls short of every single expectation for him? Thank the gods they blessed Egypt with Thutmose as Crown Prince and not you!"

Thutmose, with new eyes, watched his father continue to berate his brother, holding his tongue. His stiff neck loosened as he swallowed the growing lump in his throat. Amenhotep's shoulders grew smaller, as if to hide from their father. He had seen this same scene many times before, but this time, it made him sick. His pride at being the favored one, now only gave way to a deep hollowness in his heart. His body ached for his brother.

"I also heard you did not partake of my Sed Festival?

And now you forsake the Festival of Kaherka?" Pharaoh continued.

Amenhotep's jaw dropped before he blurted, "Did he tell you?!" He pointed at Thutmose.

"Your sister, Nebetah, told of your transgressions," Pharaoh said as his nostrils flared. "And now you dare insult the Crown Prince?"

Amenhotep's glare vanished; his gaze dropped to the floor.

"You, ignorant child," Pharaoh repeated in a whisper. "You will respect the position of Pharaoh. You never accuse the Crown Prince." He jerked his body away and cursed under his breath. "I should have your mouth stitched together for the better of Egypt." He smoothed his golden interwoven linen robes as if calming himself. Stretching out his fingers to release the final bout of anger, he took a deep breath. "Now, I came to speak to your brother, so Amenhotep, why don't you make yourself useful and learn something or attempt archery again?" He shooed him away with a flick of his finger.

Amenhotep wiped his tears from his face with his forearm.

Pharaoh groaned; his fingers curled into fists. "We are almost a man, aren't we? Well, the Crown Prince is. You may be close in years, but you are *far* from manhood. Amun, be with me, Amenhotep. There are days I doubt you will ever become a man."

Thutmose felt a weight drop to the pit of his stomach imagining what his life would be like if his father, this great King, had told him the things he told Amenhotep.

His brother bit his lip and tried to blink back his tears as Pharaoh turned from him to Thutmose. "My son, you will accompany me at the Raising of the Djed Pillar at the end of the Festival of Kaherka to show not only my strength but to signify your future as well."

Thutmose nodded his head, unable to speak. His father smiled at him, but still apparently flustered. Then, he patted his shoulder and left. Thutmose had honor bestowed upon him like every Pharaoh gave his son. He looked to Amenhotep, who gave him a pitiful glare before running off.

He rubbed his neck and remembered his mother's and Nefertiti's words before following Amenhotep.

"What do you want?" Amenhotep yelled after a while of chase. His flustered face gave rise to red eyes.

A rush of words halted behind Thutmose's lips as he stared into Amenhotep's eyes. All of the hateful moments and snide comments drowned his memories. His legs and stomach became hard as the cold of the day seeped deep into his bones. For the first time, he *saw* his brother.

"Have you come to mock me again?" Amenhotep's voice pitched higher as he tried to catch his breath. Thutmose could only give a slight shake of head, as his tongue, body and mind could not decide the words to speak or actions to take: beg his brother's forgiveness on his knees, lay out every transgression with tears... "Oh, look, he can't even shoot an arrow. Oh, look, Amenhotep cannot remember the priests' chant. Let's laugh at Amenhotep who can't–"

Thutmose swept his younger brother into a wide embrace, encircling his arms around his long, thin frame.

Amenhotep stood like a statue until he pushed Thutmose away. "Is this a new trick? A new game?" He shoved his shoulder. "Just leave me be."

"It's no trick, brother." Thutmose said with a wavering smile and a whisper as his chest tightened around his heart.

Amenhotep wrinkled his nose. "I don't believe you."

"My eyes have opened." Thutmose's face fell slack,

despite a quivering chin, and for the first time in a long time, he truly locked eyes with his brother. "I see now our father's folly. You are his son, and you are my brother." He took a step closer as his voice cracked. "And I can ask for no greater blessing in a brother, my only brother."

Amenhotep stayed silent for a long time, his chest rising and falling until he pushed his head into Thutmose's chest and wrapped his arms tight around his back. With a hitched breath, he whispered, "All I ever wanted was your and Father's love."

Thutmose finally saw Amenhotep in a way he had never done before. "From today on, you have my love...my brother." Tears welled in his eyes as he spoke. "Please forgive me for all that I have done to you."

Amenhotep's eyes drew tight. Thutmose felt the nod of his head against his chest and then squeezed his arms around him. A wave of peace flooded his heart, and he knew Bastet granted his mother's prayers after all these years.

The royal family and the nobles made their way to the city of Dedju to observe the Raising of the Djed Pillar, the symbol of resurrection of Osiris and his blessings of stability in the coming abundant crop. On the chilly winter day, the last of the Festival of Kaherka came and the priests carried their labor of devotion, the great Djed Pillar, to the House of Osiris. The royal family and the noble men, women and children wore heavy linen cloaks lined with faience, jewels and gold to keep safe from the Nile's chilly winds.

Thutmose had found Nefertiti and pulled her along to join him and his siblings before the raising began. He ran his fingers along hers, but her fingers fell limp in his hand.

He dropped his head remembering his rudeness to her. *Pharaoh does not apologize, but the Crown Prince can*, he thought and leaned his shoulder to hers. "You were right. I was wrong. A wise man listens."

Her eyes found his and danced as a smile grew on her face.

"I already choose you for my wife." He squeezed her hand. "When the time comes, I hope you accept. You will make a wise and great queen, my Nefertiti."

Her face glowed in the rising sun. "I choose you, too, my wise Crown Prince, my Thutmose."

He kissed her forehead before anyone could see, and they hid their blushes from view.

As the priests placed the pillar into its base, Pharaoh motioned for Thutmose to join him with a warm smile. He nodded and then squeezed Nefertiti's hand one more time before looking to his brother standing next to him.

"You will be a great King," Amenhotep whispered.

"Only because *you* are a patient brother," Thutmose patted Amenhotep's back and smiled.

Amenhotep grinned and nodded his head in appreciation.

As Thutmose ascended to where his father stood, he thought, *I will take care of you, my brother, for all of my days.*

ABOUT THE AUTHOR

Lauren Lee Merewether, a historical drama fiction author, loves bringing the world stories forgotten by time, filled with characters who love and lose, fight wrong with right, and feel hope in times of despair.

A lover of ancient history where mysteries still abound, Lauren loves to research overlooked, under-appreciated and relatively unknown tidbits of the past and craft for her readers engaging stories.

If you want to continue this story, check out Lauren's highly rated debut series, The Lost Pharaoh Chronicles. Start with *Book One: Salvation in the Sun.*

www.LaurenLeeMerewether.com

Facebook: @LLMBooks
Twitter: @LLMBooks

THE GIRL IN THE MIRROR

Contemporary Fiction

JOY MONETTE

Edited by
Joy Sephton

IT's icy and enchanting outside, warm and humid in here. The long mirror is grey with steam from the bath, and with my towel, I wipe it into colors again. I smile into it because I feel good. It's been mine since I was a child and was my grandmother's long ago.

This mirror has seen many things.

It saw me while I was growing up—

—Christmas. Again. The long mirror is grey with steam, and I'm glad. When it's clear, if I look into it, I see me.

I try to ignore it as I float in the bathwater, my body so thin that it rises unbidden, like a fallen branch. I look down its length, past my nearly flat boy-chest to my toes. *I wish I could love you.* But I know it doesn't hear. Tears slip out of my eyes to join the steaming water.

Showering is simpler, because I don't have to see, but baths are warm hugs and some days I cannot resist. Until I see how my hip bones stick up, and it makes me hurt with sadness. I get out because I can't stand it anymore.

Maybe one day, when I get this right, when I finally stop dreaming nightmares about food, when food becomes nothing to me, and I need nothing to do with it, maybe then I'll look okay. Perhaps then I'll look in the mirror and see a nice girl. A girl who knows how to smile—instead of smirking with a twisted mouth full of pain it cannot spit out.

I stare at my clothes for the longest time. If I wear something that fits, there'll be endless accusations. How thin you are. You must eat more. You're not getting funny teenage ideas about your weight, are you?

Christmas Day will suddenly be about me.

So it has to be the Christmas sweater, the old one that

I've carefully stretched, now several sizes too big. I'll be too hot, but that's a small price to pay. I put my bra on backward, to flatten the swelling that persists where my breasts shouldn't be. A skirt, not jeans. Long, flowing skirt so my knees and calves and ankles don't show enough bones to start a conversation. I fear that if they see me, they'll say what I know they think of me. The girl who takes up too much space.

And now I'm late and will be the focus of attention.

I can't get anything right.

I go downstairs to greet uncle, aunt, and cousins. They arrived a short while ago, but their cheeks are still red and cool, their voices happy with Christmas. Hugs and empty words. You look wonderful. My, how they've grown. Nothing much about me and nothing about my bones. Thank God, I've passed that test.

Sit at the corner of the table, on the chair that's been squeezed in where no chair belongs. If it's less crowded, I'll not be so obvious.

I'm afraid of eyes watching me: did she take enough food? Christmas food, so sad—so nostalgic. I remember the days long ago when I could eat turkey, caramel potatoes, sweet, cinnamony pumpkin, and gingerbread trifle, all without a second thought. It seems I cannot go back to that, so why invite trouble by standing out?

If I pile lots on my plate, they'll lose interest because they don't want to know how carefully and watchfully I'll transfer the food, one bite at a time, into my Christmas paper napkin. Thanking God for the manners my mother taught. Always wipe your mouth before you sip your drink. Each wipe is a mouthful of food transferred to the napkin.

Please pour me some water to sip after every bite. Water,

so clear and uncomplicated. I don't want fruit juice or any of those you're-nearly-sixteen-anyway half-glasses of wine.

Choose the food carefully; nothing soggy, nothing that might fall to bits. Take carrots, not peas. Roast potatoes, not mashed. So much food is on my plate. I will need the water.

Don't chew; just slip it into the napkin. One wipe and one sip at a time. Another napkin waits open on my lap. Passing food from red paper napkin to red paper napkin.

How much starving will it take to make me be like my cousins? Pretty, confident, able to talk as they load their forks, able to smile while they swallow. This eating in public disgusts me, but only when a fat person does it. Only when I do it.

Now I've been too greedy; the food refuses to fit into the napkin on my lap. Why do I do this—take too much food, even though it sickens me? Even though I would die before I would eat it. I sit, terrified because if I lose too much time, they will wait politely. Watch until I empty my plate. I have almost called my bluff while calling theirs.

But they won't catch me out, because when my life depends upon it, I can be more sneaky than they dare to know. Time has taught me, so I've left the turkey for last. No gravy, no cranberry sauce. I slide it off my lap to the dog who's learned to wait for gluttonous me.

I carry my plate and the bursting napkin to the kitchen. Drop Christmas dinner into the trash. Leave the napkin on top, so no one sees the food. That could cause a disaster, except no-one would care to believe it.

I'm ready for the challenge of dessert. Get a clean red paper napkin; I've mislaid mine. Stick to the steamed Christmas pudding, solid and easy to hide. Thank you, but I don't like trifle. Not anymore.

Wait for it to cool. Discard.

At last, it's almost over, just one big hurdle to go; time for family photos. I wish I were a girl who knows how to smile. I can only grimace into the camera. I don't want to see myself, and I can't bear for others to see me either. I don't want to be preserved, posted on Twitter, posted on Instagram. Let me be invisible. Besides, when I see the photos, my heart breaks for the face that doesn't know how to look happy.

I stand behind my uncle while the pictures are taken, then there's the hugging, and car doors slamming. Christmas is over now, except for the cleaning up. This, I can do, unless there's Christmassy talk. My heart is too sore for that.

It seems like hours, then I say I'm sleepy and I head for bed. But I'm not. I simply have no energy left. It's exhausting to be with people. Exhausting to wear these hot, baggy clothes. Exhausting to chase food around my plate and into a napkin. Exhausting to be incessantly sipping water. Exhausting to be so ugly.

And Christmas makes everything much, much harder.

I avoid the mirror as I brush my teeth, slip into baggy pajamas, and slide into the warm, electric-blanket bed. But it's not me that's cold. It's my heart.

My body makes a long lump under the covers. Taking up too much space.

The cat lies next to me, purring. I wish I could purr. Her short, white fur fits perfectly, and she feels no need to stretch it to hide her bones.

I fall asleep and dream my relentless nightmares. Food chasing me. Food to slow me down, blow me up like a party balloon, make me fill the mirror. Food that I want to throw up.

Then I dream about me. Seeing myself in the mirror, and when I do, a spasm of pain flashes deep into my soul and stays there. Such a sad, hateful girl. There's too much of her, and there's no one who loves her. No one at all; she doesn't even love herself.

I wake up sweating, silently weeping.

The wintry days go by, stretching endlessly before me. Days of imitating happy and hiding my collar bones. Every day is winter to me as I bundle my sweating body into heavy, loose-fitting clothes. Every day is winter because the coldness doesn't leave my heart.

The energy I need is enormous, and however hard I try, I can't be invisible to me. And however hard I try, I cannot take up no space.

I hate me.

There, I've said it.

Another Christmas. It's a time for giving, but it always seems to take, take, take.

The difference this year, as I fake the traditions, is that I found someone to talk to. Just once a week. Someone who, I'm learning, doesn't care about the space I take up, or if I say nothing for the forty minutes we're together. This kind of *doesn't care* is empowering.

My parents don't know; I used a free government phone number to make an appointment. They don't deserve to know.

Truth is, I'm afraid for them to know.

Somehow, I survive this Christmas Day, but it was just as painful, just as exhausting. I have even more bones than I did last year, and I avoid the mirror as always. My body is still an ugly lump beneath the covers, still taking up too much space.

The cat lies next to me, soundly asleep. I wish I could sleep so soundly. She rolls and stretches—relaxed and safe —and goes back to her dreams.

My dreams are getting worse. It seems those appointments for talking are digging ugly holes, and the truth is leaking out.

I dream of my life. Of being wrong. Of not fitting in.

Dreams of huge faces circling, scornful. Girls can't do that. It's too scientific and you're not clever enough. I try to hide in the chemistry lab, but the faces follow me, lighting Bunsen burners, sloshing the cleaning alcohol. I run again, fearing an explosion, but I cannot outrun such contempt.

Dreams of huge tongues licking wet lips, mouths screeching at me. Always wear lots of clothes. It's not fair on your father. Not fair on your brothers. Not fair on all the men in the world to wear a sleeveless, short summer dress. Don't walk around in shorts asking for trouble. But I'm not asking for trouble; I'm too hot to wear jeans or a jacket. I hide in the shadows, so I don't have to sweat, but I run when I see the boys and the men getting close. I never feel safe for what they will do to me, but it never happens. I cannot relax, in case it does.

Dreams of huge hearts crawling with maggots. The world is not that way; the way you feel it is wrong. You're wrong, wrong, wrong to feel the way you do. I'm angry with myself because by now I should know that. I try to hide those lying, twisted feelings in a drawer, but they swell up and push it open and come spilling out. I cannot hide my feelings unless I hide myself.

Dreams of huge fingers pointing; you're repulsive. See those breasts swelling, those hips curving. You cannot hide; you're a growing girl, and you'll be a woman soon. You take up too much space. Huge fingers waiting to rip me into tiny pieces, to make me fit. I hear the sound of tearing, and I scream.

More and more dreams: they run into each other, too many to count.

I wake up sweating, silently weeping, and my fingers are shaking as I reach out to touch the cat.

Such a sad, hateful girl. There is too much of her, and there is no one who loves her. But now she has someone to talk to. For forty minutes, once a week.

How I despise it: Christmas Day is back.

Another winter made hot by clothes and cold by feelings. But I have someone to talk to, forty minutes a week.

Learning not to be obsessed with the mirror because it's not where the problems lie. Learning instead to look inside me, to look and see and think and describe. Discovering what makes me feel so bad. What makes me hate myself. What has created this winter in my soul. What has messed with all the space.

The talking leads to thinking.

Sitting at the Christmas table, I have too many thoughts to be good at either conversation or eating.

At night the cat kneads the covers against my back, feeling loved—even without encouragement. I wish I felt that way.

My dreams are strange, frightening, hopeful things where I take different shapes, completing heroic quests, and fighting epic battles. I am Frodo, struggling to reach Mount Doom with the One Ring. I am Lucy, clutching my cordial, racing with Aslan to war. I am Katniss, armed with my bow and arrow, my wits and Peeta's love.

I wake up exhausted, sweating, feeling wild-eyed. Shocked.

Christmas Day is back again, not entirely terrible, waiting for me to try it out like a different hairstyle. I have let go of many things, but not all of them. The most important is that I don't blame myself—not much, at least—for how I feel about the space. It has been years of talking, forty minutes a week, and then my time is up. But the talking stays in my head. Things to think about.

Our dog, Button, has stopped sitting under the table. There's not a lot there for him anymore. Not often. But our beautiful cat still sleeps with me. Her name is Zara, and she has a glossy white coat, inscrutable eyes, and a purr she knows how to use.

I lie in the bath, and my bones are there, but no longer fuel for an entire discussion. I also have tentative breasts that I'm learning to like, and my chest no longer looks like it escaped from a boy.

As I stand before the bright mirror, Zara winds herself around my legs, and I pick her up. She's warm and often cuddly, but tonight she squirms away. She wants to watch from the open wardrobe. And that's alright. I'm always surprised when I find I don't need others to love me— although I'm glad when they do. I'm working on being enough for myself.

Sometimes I still hope to find love outside of me, in a faucet or an ocean. I would feel safe drowning in love. But I have to love myself, so I can feel safe without drowning. Not loving myself is what makes me yearn for love in a faucet or even the whole big sea.

In a way, I knew these things before. But it's only now they make sense to me. And a lot of the time, what I feel for myself *is* enough. My image in the mirror, not perfect, is nice. It takes up about the right amount of space, and when I smile at the young woman there, she smiles back at me. I'm glad. I realize she's quite pretty. Sometimes I have to remind myself that she's also likable and loveable, but other times I remember without trying.

I decide what to wear: a lovely, lacy top with blue jeans. I'll be comfortable this Christmas. I might even feel pretty like me-in-the-mirror. I'll have to try that idea on for size. And, did you see that; I made a pun!

Christmas is supposed to be magical, and I can always use some magic. I've talked and looked and seen and described and thought myself into a place that enjoys the feel of magic.

Meeting people is easier when I look into myself and find the good things. People don't look at me and despise me. They don't. Most people like me as much as I like them. But every day is like test-driving that theory. And very slowly, I'm getting used to it. Learning to love myself and to let myself be loved.

I go downstairs and greet my uncle Max, my aunt Nadine, and my cousins, Sharon and Lisa. I hug them all, glad they're here. We talk and laugh, and mostly it's great. I still can't show too much of myself, but for now, that's fine.

To my surprise, Christmas dinner is delicious. Freedom and magic help me to enjoy; aromas mixing, flavors blending. This year I even mashed the potatoes.

I'm still nervous of trifle, so I'll stick to the berries. Raspberries, blackberries, red currants, they're perfect.

It's been an eternity since I enjoyed the sensation of tasting.

Much later, I climb into bed. Zara has gone out hunting, but my heart is warm, and I stretch out. It's luxurious.

I fall asleep and dream dreams I don't remember, but I'm relaxed and happy when I wake.

Every day's a challenge to overcome, but it's like that for us all. My challenge is to enjoy overcoming my challenges. Then my life will always be enjoyable ;)

See, a wink!

It's slow, but I know one day I will get this thing. Because I can take up the space I need.

Where was I?

It's Christmas Day; icy and enchanting outside, warm and humid in here. The long mirror was grey with steam, but I've wiped it alive again. I look into its brightness. I think of my gran who looked into it first.

When I was growing up, it seemed to watch me endlessly, spitefully. But now we smile together. Almost every day.

ABOUT THE AUTHOR

Joy Monette likes windmills, rain, and acacia trees. She also likes writing intriguing short stories that usually end up in the first person, but that doesn't mean all these things have actually happened to her. Just some of them—like eating disorders. She's also writing her First Big Novel, which is taking a great deal longer than the short stories. Other than that, she lives in Johannesburg, South Africa, so when it's winter in some places, it's summer in hers.

www.joymonette.com

THE OUTSIDER

Fantasy, Myths and Legends

LEIGH ROBERTS

Edited by
Joy Sephton

IT WAS MEALTIME, and Oh'Dar sat on the cold stone bench with his adopted family. He pushed his food around in front of him with one finger, uninterested. The others were engaged in start-of-day conversation to which he was only half listening. He picked up a piece of broccoli, chewed it mindlessly, and swallowed. His mother, the only mother he had ever known, looked over at him, her dark brown eyes filled with love. She reached over and rubbed his back, jostling him gently. She smelled of lavender, ginger, soapwort, and the other herbs and plants she used as the community Healer.

His earliest memory was of those eyes, of her leaning over him, smiling at him like that. Her eyes were always kind; her embrace strong, yet tender. He couldn't remember her giving him strict correction, only gentle redirection, lots of encouragement, and gentle hugs.

Those early years were easy. He was surrounded by love and support. The adult females of the community accepted him and overlooked his differences. *All children are innocent and to be loved. No matter how different.* But, as his circle had widened, so had Oh'Dar's understanding of his situation among the People of the High Rocks.

He knew that his mother had rescued him, a Waschini Outsider, when he was an infant; human survivor of a terrible massacre she had stumbled across. Contact with Outsiders was forbidden, and going so far as to bring an Outsider into the People's ancient secluded Sasquatch community had caused great hardship for her. He had only learned this relatively recently, and he realized that during his childhood, she had done everything she could to shield him from adult talk and adult issues.

Oh'Dar finished eating, got up and left the table, his brother joining him.

"Are you listening to me?"

"No, I'm sorry. I was not. What did you say, Nootau?"

"Come out with us today. The new snow has fallen. We want to go down to the Great River and practice skipping stones."

"Who is going?" asked Oh'Dar.

"Raulk, Petraea, Istas. Kahrok. Maybe Kyqat, Zsorn, I don't know."

"Istas?"

"Yes, why? Females can go too," Nootau said.

"I *know that*. Never mind, go on without me."

In that moment it dawned on Nootau that perhaps Oh'Dar liked Istas and he immediately felt bad for his brother. He knew that Istas might be nice to Oh'Dar, but that she would never consider him for anything but a friend. Until now, Nootau had never considered whether Oh'Dar would ever find a mate once he was an adult. He would never be the strong protector and provider that the females expected. Nootau had gotten past seeing Oh'Dar's differences. He was just Oh'Dar, not one of the Outsiders.

"Come on. Come with us for once."

"Kahrok is going? He doesn't like me."

"He might not even come. Don't let that *PetaQ* get to you."

"You better not let Mama hear you use that language."

"I know," Nootau smiled. "Okay, but if you are not going, I am not going. Let's find something to do together."

Oh'Dar stopped to think, looking at his brother while he thought the situation over. Fast approaching maturity, like the rest of the group, Nootau was clearly going to be one of the larger males in the community. His already broadening rib cage, his biceps, and thighs hinted at the strength and contour to come. He was no doubt going to have the same robust build as their father. Nobody knew who Oh'Dar's real father was – or his real mother, for that matter, either. This was all he had ever known. He could not imagine anything different.

"All right, I will go with you to the Great River. Give me a few minutes to go and put on something warmer. I will meet you at the Great Entrance in a bit."

When he reached the meeting place, Oh'Dar was disappointed to see that Kahrok had indeed joined the group. Oh'Dar decided to ignore him and try to put the young male's presence out of his mind. Kahrok had a bit of a mean streak, and Oh'Dar seemed to bring it out in him.

Once assembled and ready, the group headed down the rocky slope to the Great River. Nootau took the lead, purposefully slowing everyone else up so that Oh'Dar would not be left behind. Oh'Dar always took up the rear. It was safer; should any of the others take a tumble, he needed to be behind them. He could be seriously hurt if caught in their way. His foot coverings made it more treacherous, another disadvantage because the others did not need them.

The soft, new snow blanketed everything. Clumps of the white powder dusted all the bare branches, as well as the soft needles of the dark green firs. The Cardinals chip-chipped at them from above, hopping from one branch to another. A red squirrel, fat and ready for winter, barked at them from overhead. The cold air stung Oh'Dar's nose.

It was slow going, but they had finally negotiated nearly all of the snowy path when suddenly the forward movement stopped, and there was a commotion at the front.

"Quit going so slow. I know what you're doing, Nootau. You're holding us all up because of your so-called *brother*," griped Kahrok.

"If you are in such a hurry, go on ahead," Nootau snapped back.

"You know what? Forget it. I have better things to do than hang out with you and that Outsider runt. He doesn't belong here. He can't keep up. And he is always wrapped up in that ridiculous clump of hides."

"You had better stop there, Kahrok. Your father would be very disappointed to hear you talk like this. Oh'Dar is one of us. And he is not a runt. His kind is just different, that's all. You need to take it back."

"Take what back? It's the truth. Look at him." Kahrok pointed back at Oh'Dar, standing farther up on the path.

"Why, I bet I could pick him up with one hand," and Kahrok started towards Oh'Dar.

Nootau quickly moved around Kahrok and blocked his way. Nootau had nothing to fear from the likes of Kahrok, and although always quick to protect his puny brother, he knew it wasn't the same as Oh'Dar being able to do it himself. He worried he could not be everywhere with Oh'Dar, all the time.

"That's enough."

Kahrok looked him up and down. "What are you going to do? Tell your father, the *great High Protector*, Acaraho?"

"No. I will take care of this with you myself." Nootau, standing taller, glared at Kahrok. Time ticked by. Nobody moved.

Oh'Dar could see there had been some type of altercation going on between his brother and Kahrok that now looked like it had turned into a standoff. Kahrok seemed to be sizing up Nootau—who for a young male *was* looking pretty formidable.

"What's going to happen when he doesn't have you to hide behind, Nootau? I'm leaving." Kahrok turned around and started back up the hill. As he brushed past Oh'Dar, he sneered and whispered, "*Waschini PetaQ*," revealing his sharp canines.

Nootau was right behind him and took hold of Oh'Dar's arm to get his brother's attention away from Kahrok.

"Come on; we're almost all the way down."

"What was that about? Me, right?" Oh'Dar felt a sinking feeling in his stomach. More than anything, he just wanted to go back inside and hide from everyone.

"You know Kharok always has to have some issue."

"It looked like you two were about to start fighting."

"I was ready. But he backed down. It's a good thing because if either of our parents found out, there would be *krell* to pay."

Oh'Dar nodded. The People did not tolerate bullying, insulting, or other forms of improper behavior.

The group started moving again, and before long they stood together on the bank, a safe distance from the swiftly moving waters of the Great River churning by in front of them. Oh'Dar breathed deeply of the crisp, sharp air: it was refreshing, and he was warm enough to enjoy the cold weather. He envied the fact that the others required nothing beyond their light down under covering and thick body hair. He pulled the hides around him against a sudden icy gust of wind.

He was relieved that Istas had not joined them and heard whatever other insults Kahrok might have come up with. Now he could relax and at least try to have a good time. He also wouldn't have to worry about doing something stupid that would remind her how much weaker he was than the other males.

It was not Oh'Dar's imagination. He *was* far weaker than any of the males in his community. In every physical way, he was inferior compared to the others. Shorter, frail, with lanky, pale limbs. His nails were neither thick nor strong—useless for clawing or gouging or ripping things open. He lacked the large, sharp canines of the others. He could not hear half the sounds they did. He was not able to pick out the smell of an elk from a deer, a coyote from a wolf. In the dark, he stumbled and fell, whereas they could still see well enough to cope just fine. He could not travel to the lower levels of their sprawling underground home cave, Kthama, without carrying a phosphorescent stone, because there was not enough light for him to navigate. He felt the cold, so he always had to wear coverings of some type, even on the first level of Kthama. The only time he didn't feel cold was during the height of summer. When the others were suffering from the heat, he was comfortable, and at least for a while could lose the wraps of hide and fur.

When he was a child, his world had been confined to his mother, the People's Healer; her assistant, Nadiwani, who was also helping raise him, and a small collection of others. He was only allowed to join in with the others far later than any of his peers. His mother would not risk it earlier for fear they would unintentionally hurt him.

"The waters are too rough," Raulk proclaimed. "But we can go to one of the smaller ponds."

The water doesn't bother me, thought Oh'Dar.

One of the few things Oh'Dar excelled at and could do better than any of the People, of any age, was that he loved water, and had become an expert swimmer. His peers were reluctant even to get wet.

And it was just after a swim, a short while ago, that it had hit him just how different he truly was. That he would never really be one of them.

He and the male he had always thought of as his father, the High Protector of the People of the High Rocks, had been sitting on the bank in Oh'Dar's favorite spot, his first choice for fishing or playing around in the warm shallow waters. The scent of wildflowers filled the air. The rays of the sun in the bright sky overhead warmed him after his swim. He let his feet dangle in the water. If he sat there long enough, the fish would come up and nibble at his toes, which tickled and felt good. As the two sat talking, Oh'Dar noticed their reflections, side by side in the still waters. He looked. He looked again.

"What is it, son?" his father asked, wondering what he was staring at.

Oh'Dar didn't answer. Instead, he paddled his feet briskly, as if the ripples that dispelled the image would make the hard truth of it go away too. Later that day, in the quiet moments before sleep, he let the full force of the realization hit him, mortified that at his age tears were sliding down his cheeks and soaking into the soft sleeping mat beneath him. *I will never fit in. I will never really be one of the People.*

He eventually told his father what had bothered him that day. The High Protector did not try to tell Oh'Dar otherwise; instead, he was straightforward. "It is true, Oh'Dar. You are different. But you will find your place. Do not compare yourself with your brother or your peers. Different is not bad. Our differences make us stronger. It is just a matter of honoring and recognizing them. You have gifts the others do not have, though you do not realize it yet."

The words of his father were kind and wise, as always, but Oh'Dar knew that parents' words were biased by their love for their offspring. Oh'Dar tried to stop comparing his own abilities to others'. Sometimes he could do it; most times, he could not.

Oh'Dar brought his thoughts back to the moment.

"It's too rough. We can't skip stones here. Let's go find one of the quieter streams," Nootau was saying.

As they turned to leave, movement in one of the huge oak trees leaning over the Great River caught Raulk's eye.

Up on one of the limbs that stretched low over the river, was a Bobcat. Behind her were two kittens, tiny fluff balls just learning to climb. Raulk pointed, and the others looked up and spotted them also.

Oh'Dar's mouth hung open. He could swear one of the kittens was white. "Is that a *white* Bobcat kit?" he exclaimed.

It was true. The others stared in amazement with him.

The People revered all the creations of the Great Spirit, especially her forest creatures. They lived in harmony with all, generation after generation. If something had to die, they dispatched it quickly and mercifully, then thanked it for its sacrifice. But white creatures were never intentionally killed. Usually, they were deer or birds; but whatever they were, white coloring was considered sacred.

"I have never heard of a white Bobcat before," said Nootau, shielding his eyes with his palm and squinting upward. The others nodded their agreement. Oh'Dar wished his mother was here to see this. With her highly developed Healer's seventh sense, she would perhaps know if this were a sign, and be able to interpret its meaning.

As they stood there watching, the white kitten scrambled between its mother's feet and out to the end of the branch. They looked on in horror as it slipped, hanging precariously by its front claws.

"Oh, no!" they all shouted in unison, and at that moment the kitten dropped toward the churning waters of the Great River below.

They all rushed closer to the edge of the bank, sick to their stomachs at the loss of something so precious, white or not.

But there in the middle of the rolling waters was the little kit—luckily alive, but its situation still dire—now stranded on a large rock in the middle of the moving current.

Their joy at seeing it still alive was immediately crushed.

"There is no way to get to it. It is going to die!" exclaimed Zsorn. They looked at each other helplessly, none of them capable of safely breaching the waters to save the kitten.

Oh'Dar paused a moment, then proclaimed, "No, it's not going to die." Forgetting his insecurities, he shouted, "Quick, someone run back and get the longest woven lashing you can find. There's one piled in the corner of the Guard's station in the Great Entrance."

Running was one of the things the People did best. They were frighteningly quick. Without Oh'Dar to slow them down earlier, they could easily have reached the Great River in minutes rather than nearly half an hour. Within what seemed like seconds, Nootau was back with the long, thick cord.

Oh'Dar quickly ran it through his hands, checking the length. He then coiled the rope and slid it over one shoulder, so it draped across his body. Ready, he made a beeline towards the large oak that leaned over the water.

"Are you crazy!" yelled Nootau as he realized what his brother was about to do.

Nootau is supposed to make sure I am safe; he will never get over it if I make a mistake and get hurt—or worse. But I cannot let that little creature die. I have to try.

Before they knew it, Oh'Dar was up the tree and inching his way along the limb. It could never have held the weight of any one of the others, but it was bearing his without complaint.

The mother Bobcat, with her second kitten, had come down the tree and was pacing the bank.

"Come on!" said Nootau, and he quickly led the others to the base of the great oak. He motioned, and they each took up a place, standing guard around the trunk. The Bobcat hissed and growled in complaint, but she was no match for the group of Sasquatch males and backed away. If she had any idea of climbing up after Oh'Dar, the thought was put from her mind.

When he was in position over the mewing kitten, Oh'Dar secured the rope to the branch and tied the other end around his waist. Down below in the powdered snow, the mother Bobcat was now screaming her desperation.

Oh'Dar tested his knot and carefully lowered himself, the whole time keeping an eye on the tiny white creature. If it slipped off the rock, he was prepared to drop into the waters to save it, trusting the rope and his swimming skills to keep them both from being washed downstream.

His feet found purchase on the icy, wet rock and within seconds he had scooped up the tiny white bundle of fur. It was damp from the spray and terribly frightened. Fortunately, it was too little to scratch him much, and he tucked it safely inside his thick wraps, making sure it could not fall out. The warmth of his body must have been soothing, as it settled down quicker than he thought it would. Satisfied it was secure, he prepared to pull himself back up the rope.

Oh'Dar might have been frail compared to the others, but for his own build, he was strong. Hand over hand, he climbed as the others watched, each holding his breath.

Finally, Oh'Dar hoisted himself up enough to get a leg over the branch, and was soon safely back on top of it. Checking again that the kitten was secure, he untied himself and made his way back to the trunk of the tree, and from there, safely to the ground.

The others gathered around him as he pulled the little Bobcat kitten out from inside his wraps.

"You just used up your first life," Oh'Dar joked, holding her out in front of him. No longer quite as frightened, she now hissed and spat ungratefully at him, trying her best to look as fierce as possible. He ignored the protestations and dried her as much as he could with the edge of his hide tunic.

Then he walked around to where the mother Bobcat was eyeing them warily. Making sure she could see her mother and her littermate, he set the kitten on the ground. She shook her head, then ran to her mama. They watched as she greeted her kitten, licking it and rolling the little thing over on its back to check it out.

Nootau and the others encircled Oh'Dar and praised him.

"That was amazing. None of us could have done that. Thank the Great Spirit you came with us today," said Kyqat.

"I can't wait to tell everyone what you did!" exclaimed Nootau, glad to have something with which to build up his brother's self-esteem.

An unfamiliar feeling came over Oh'Dar. For the first time, he could see he had value. And for the first time, he felt as if he might find a way to belong. His father's words came back to him: *Differences are not bad. Our differences make us stronger.*

"We did it together. You ran and got the rope, Nootau. And all of you protected me from the Bobcat while I was rescuing her kitten."

"What a way to start the day," said Raulk.

"So, who is ready to go skip some rocks?" asked Oh'Dar.

As the others turned to walk away, Oh'Dar caught the tail end of the mother Bobcat and her kits disappearing into the edge of the woods.

"I wonder if I will ever see Kaishee again," he mused.

"You named it?" chuckled Zsorn. "And how do you know it is a female?"

"I peeked while I was stuffing her into my tunic," he said. They laughed.

"And yes, I did name her. And I hope to see her again someday."

A couple of his friends patted him gingerly on the back, and then they all walked away together amid smiles and laughter, in search of the perfect skipping stones on the first day of winter snowfall.

ABOUT THE AUTHOR

When **Leigh Roberts** is not caught up in the fantasy world of Etera with Adia, Acaraho, Oh'Dar, Nadiwani, and Khon'-Tor, she is enjoying the beauty of the rural area in which she lives.

An avid reader since early childhood, she grew up on super-hero comics, science fiction stories, and television shows like The Twilight Zone, The Outer Limits, and Star Trek.

Star Trek had a huge influence on her thinking and taught her the infinite possibilities of imagination—and how to split infinitives. Spoiler alert: you may find a Klingon word or phrase dropped in here or there.

She loves being an author, and her heart's desire is to be writing for a long, long time to come.

www.leighrobertsauthor.com

Facebook Group: The Etera Chronicles

THE LOST TRADITION

Sci Fi Dystopian

A.L. RUGOVA

A bonus scene from
The Free Prisoner
(Book One of TIAMIS series)

Edited by
Diane Shirk

THE MARKETPLACE WAS MORE BUSTLING than usual. Vendors pushed their carts full of merchandise around, hollering at passersby. Townspeople strolled along the square and streets, stopping occasionally for a small bite or to look at interesting craftwork.

Despite the blazing sun, the cool air of December had made the shopping experience pleasant and relaxing for all.

All except for two.

"Do you—do you have to run—so fast," Kevin panted as he bent over to catch his breath, his hand pressing on his side.

Canti ignored him. "Bula, Api. Two lamb curry, please —" she huffed, big beads of sweat on her forehead and nose.

"Bula, Miss Canti," Api said and smiled apologetically. The old man was wearing his usual strange-patterned shirt with a calf-length black cloth tied around his waist. "I'm sorry you have to chase after me every time. How about this? I'll stay here from two to three every day. Just for you!"

"That—that would be wonderful." Kevin slowly straightened himself up, his lungs still burning.

If Canti was going to sprint like a loose dog every time they visited the marketplace, he would either become a skilled marathon runner or dead meat.

Api opened the lid of his pot. The exotic aroma rushed in their faces, and Kevin immediately forgot all about the throbbing pain in his side.

"Rice or roti?"

"Rice!" Canti and Kevin said almost in harmony.

Suddenly, Canti gasped.

"What? You lost your coins?" Kevin asked.

"No. Look!"

A white feline jumped onto Api's shoulder and curled up behind his neck. It sniffed the curry and meowed.

Api chuckled. "You rascal. You know I can't feed you curry; it will burn your little tongue."

The feline brushed its tail against Api's cheek before it leaped off and ran into the bustling square. Canti took a step forward. Kevin grabbed her wrist.

"No. You. Don't," Kevin hissed.

"Beautiful cat, isn't it? We have lots of cats here, but none is as spotless as that one. It's as white as snow," Api said.

"Snow..." Canti whispered underneath her breath.

"What was that you said? Ah, lamb. Coming up!"

As Api poured the yellow, rich, and creamy liquid on top of the rice, Kevin couldn't help but take a deep breath again. The burning sensation in his lungs had finally disappeared.

"Here, two lamb curry with rice. No, no need. It's on me."

"Huh?" Canti stopped mid-action as she was reaching into her pocket for coins.

"We appreciate the offer, Api," Kevin quickly recovered. "But we can't simply—"

"Take it as my apology for making you guys run all the way. Also..." Api said as he shoved the two wooden containers into Kevin's hands. "*Marau na Kerisimasi.*"

"Mala la what?" Kevin blurted.

"*Marau na Kerisimasi.*" Api chuckled. "It means 'Merry Christmas.'"

He left and greeted the other customers who were lured in by the exotic aroma of his curry, leaving Kevin and Canti standing in confusion.

"WHAT DID YOU SAY?"

The entire kitchen staff fell quiet, stopped their tasks, and stared at Bob the chef and Kevin with great interest.

"I said, 'I want a Christmas party for Canti,'" Kevin said and then quickly added, "please."

He suppressed the urge to wince as he could feel the dull pain lingering in his head.

What a drag.

It's not like he had a choice. He did not come up with the idea of a Christmas party.

Heck, he didn't even know what Christmas was.

After they had left Api to his business, Canti bombarded him with questions about Christmas. When she was finally convinced that Kevin had zero idea what Christmas was, she headed straight to the study room as soon as they returned to the mansion.

Forty minutes later, right when Kevin stretched out his legs on the couch, ready to enjoy some alone time with a book, a heavy object landed solidly on the top of his head.

Turned out Canti had found information about this Christmas thing in an ancient encyclopedia. She could care less about the lump she had just bestowed upon Kevin's scalp as she chattered excitedly about her discovery.

The colorful pictures of bright decorations and delicious food grasped Kevin's attention immediately and caused him to forget about the pain and anger.

They imagined what the mansion would look like if tiny little starlights were hung around the roof. They talked about decorating all the pine trees in the forest. Canti suggested assigning each floating island a festive color and lighting up all the Inter-Island Suspension Bridges. They had so much fun, imagining crazy parties and festivals if Christmas was still celebrated here—until Canti decided to make a party happen.

"Listen here, kid." Bob slammed his knife on the cutting

board, his face red. "Ever since you came to this household uninvited—"

"I was adopted, you know."

"—A lowly nobody now claiming to be the young master—"

"Your Master adopted me. Like I had a choice!"

"—Disrupting the peace of this mansion—"

"For the record, I'm not responsible for the pranks."

"—Four kitchen maids quit their jobs and left—"

"Hey, what does that have to do with me?" Kevin protested.

"—Still we so kindly tolerate you and treat you as our young master—"

"Oh? You weren't so friendly, if I remember it right." Kevin huffed.

"—And even helped you get along with Little Miss!" Bob began yelling. "The whole purpose of getting you two on good terms is so that someone can keep an eye on Miss Canti. But turns out you're just another Simon, getting wrapped around her little finger—"

"I heard someone shouting my name. It had better be good," Simon the butler said as he staggered in, his cane creating distinct taps on the tile floor.

Bob gestured his hand toward Kevin in a big motion. "Young Master here has brought up an outrageous request."

"How outrageous?"

"Canti-wants-a-party outrageous," Kevin said light-heartedly.

"Party?"

"A Christmas party. On Christmas Eve," Bob grunted.

Simon thought for a while. "In that case, we'll put it as our priority..."

"Are you nuts?" Bob shouted. "That's in two days! There's

no way we can pull it off. Somebody talk some sense into her!"

"I tried. And failed. You think it's easy to reason with an eight-year-old?" Kevin said darkly.

"Then get my sister! Surely she will know how to—"

"I heard Little Miss wants a party. That sounds like fun."

Everyone turned their attention to the kitchen door. Helena had just walked in, her mood brighter than usual.

"A Christmas party on Christmas Eve," Bob said to Helena, almost pleading. "Are you aware that it's in two days?"

"Well, we'll just have to set it as our priority, won't we? Starting now. Master Tama seems interested, so he's given permission."

Bob stared at Helena incredulously. He turned and walked back to his station, his shoulders slumped in defeat. "I'll whip out a party menu," he muttered.

There was no time to lose. If Canti wanted a party, there must be a party.

And if she requested a Christmas party, it'd better look like a Christmas party. Even though Kevin had no idea what Christmas was all about, he knew right away that decorations were one of those things to set the mood right. He collected a bunch of pine branches and pinecones and headed for the third greenhouse.

"And that's why you came? To ask me to make a wreath?" Old FuYong raised her cane and whacked it on Kevin's head. "I am the chief pharmacologist and healer of this kingdom! How dare you treat me like a Christmas elf? Teenagers are the worst, there's one fact that will never change even after a millennium—"

Under normal circumstances, Kevin would have dodged away with ease. But this greenhouse was full of toxic plants; one curious touch might be enough to unleash a horrific rash all over his body.

Kevin let the petite, yet feisty, ninety-year-old beat him and shriek at him until exhausted. Fortunately, it didn't take long.

"Hmph! All this trouble for a holiday that's long forgotten. Your Little Miss is just as reckless as usual."

Though spitting bitter words, Old FuYong skillfully trimmed the branches, leaves, and cones for the wreath. In return, Kevin volunteered to sweep the floor.

"Why is it forgotten? It sure looks like a cheerful holiday."

"Banned," Old FuYong said.

"Banned? When? For what?"

"It was banned long before Earth fell apart. Because it's a religious holiday."

Kevin's head tilted sideways in confusion. The old woman sighed and continued.

"In the old world, each country or kingdom had two organizations to keep its citizens in check: religion and government. Both were in a constant fight to gain authority over the other. And different religious groups couldn't get along, either. Soon the politicians and world leaders took advantage of their quarrels and banned all religious practice permanently."

Kevin resumed sweeping in silence, contemplating the historical fact that Old FuYong had just told him.

One day, he would rule his empire, and thus he had been taught the philosophies and principles of a ruler. He had always been warned how a ruler's selfish desire could bring damage to the entire kingdom, and the effect could last for generations.

Kevin thought about the beautiful pictures in the encyclopedia and imagined how wondrous it would have been if all religious holidays were kept. He thought about the politicians and world leaders that were responsible for the disappearance of holidays. He wondered if those were the same cowards that had exiled his ancestors to the bleak and dreary moon.

A small fire sparked in his chest.

When he had finished sweeping the entire greenhouse, Old FuYong presented him two wreaths.

"Two?" Kevin held the wreaths in his arms; they emitted a rich piney scent. Maybe he should have cleaned the glass windows, too.

"You brought so much material. Might as well," the old woman grumbled. "*Sheng Dan Kuai Le*."

"Huh?"

"Nothing. Outta here!"

The massive Red Moon sat faithfully in the west, assuring travelers that they would never be lost. Its rusty red hue glowed brightly in the sunset.

"Say, why do we have to be out here?" Canti pouted. "The party is starting in two hours."

"I can't let you ruin the preparations, can I? You're way too excited. Besides, you need to wait for the magic to happen."

"But I want to *see* the magic happen!"

Kevin sighed and chuckled. Canti was too much for him

to handle. He leaned against the rail, rested his chin on his forearms, and stared at the view in front of him. Seeing she couldn't get more of a response from him, Canti humphed and copied Kevin.

Usually, only the top half of the Red Moon was visible above the landscape. As they stood on the Inter-Island Suspension Bridge, with no obstacles before them, the core of the dead Earth floated in front of their very eyes, emitting a rusty red glow. Soft, icy clouds brushed past their cheeks occasionally.

Canti sighed. "If only we could put lights on this bridge..."

"Not likely. That would pose way too much potential safety concerns. What if things fall down and into the kingdoms below us?"

"It's no fun!" Canti finally yelled. "I can't even do anything. There's nothing for me to do. They won't even let us enjoy the view in peace!"

Kevin glanced to his left and right. They were standing in the middle of the bridge. One soldier positioned six feet away from them on both sides.

"You have no right to complain. You've brought this on yourself, remember?"

She fell silent. Of course, she had better not forget. After all, Canti was the one who had pushed him off the bridge one time. Though their astro-garment had initiated the floating function successfully, a rescuing ship had been dispatched to retrieve them. An ambassador and a special cleaning squad had also been sent to a kingdom right below them, because Kevin's vomit had so unfortunately landed on a noble's head.

After a brief silence, Canti softly said, "Those pictures in the book...most of them have snow in them."

"It would seem so."

"Did it snow in December in the old world?"

"I think there were some places that didn't."

"I really want to see snow. It's so white and so pretty. Is snow really as white as that cat in the marketplace?"

"Ha ha. Much whiter. The cat would seem gray if you threw it into the snow."

"Really? What about the White Moon?"

A moving scene of a white street flashed in front of Kevin's eyes. Stone houses and pavements covered in snow. Red, pink, and white plum blossom petals twirled in the wind. The snow glittered and stung his eyes just by imagining it.

"You would think the cat was a chunk of charcoal," Kevin stated brutally.

"Wow, and I thought the cat was super white already..."

Canti fell silent again and drifted into her imaginary wonderland. Not willing to be intoxicated with nostalgia and sorrow, Kevin cleared his throat.

"We still have one hour until the party starts. Wanna walk around the marketplace? But don't eat too many snacks," Kevin warned as he saw the glinting in Canti's eyes. "Don't blame me if you end up not having enough room for Christmas food."

Canti pounced on him. At first, Kevin thought she was trying to push him off the bridge again. The soldiers had also sprung into action. But she only flung her arms around his neck and cheered.

"I want hazelnut chocolates!"

❄

It was time to head home for the party. Half of the jacinth sky had been tinted with violet.

"Why aren't we going in through the front door?" Canti asked as Kevin led her around the mansion. "Why are you taking me to the—Oh!"

A white, dome-shaped canopy sat at the back of the mansion, right next to the lake. Long table runner cloths of red and gold stretched from the roof of the mansion to the top of the canopy, with tiny lights attached to them.

"Wow!" Canti sighed again as she walked into the canopy.

A broken chandelier hung from the middle of the canopy. Crystal ornaments reflected the light of a candle that was placed inside it. More red and gold satin cloths draped elegantly on the canopy legs like curtains. Delicate silverware and glassware were placed neatly on the white tablecloth.

"These utensils are reserved for super special occasions." Canti gasped but then asked, "Who else is coming? I thought this was just a small party for us."

"Why? Is aunty not welcomed here?"

Canti spun around and sprinted forward as soon as she recognized the newcomer.

"Aunty Naraya!"

Queen Naraya picked Canti up into her arms. King Edward chuckled and scanned the area. "You guys have put a lot of thought into this."

"And effort," another voice said.

Canti looked to the back door and exclaimed, "Daddy? I thought you had a late meeting!"

Tama smiled as he gestured behind him. "A meeting with a special guest."

A bald man walked through the door after Tama.

"Uncle Kava!" Canti dashed toward the bald man and gave him a hug.

"Yup, it's me. All the way from Mars." Kava grinned from ear to ear. "Happy?"

"Yes, I am! My family is all here! This is so wonderful!" Canti chirped. "*Marau na Kerisimasi!*"

Everyone stared at her in confusion, except for Kevin. "It means 'Merry Christmas.' We learned that from Api, the old man that sells Fijian curry in the marketplace," he explained.

"Fijian, huh? What is it in our ancestor's language?" Kava looked to his brother.

Tama thought for a while. "*Manuia le Kerisimasi.*"

"Really?" Kava scratched his bald head. "I could have sworn it's '*Mele Kalikimaka.*'"

Tama shrugged. "Could be both."

"*Gëzuar Krishtlindjet,*" Queen Naraya and King Edward said in unison.

"Wow, there are so many languages." Canti looked as if her brain had been overloaded with information.

"There used to be more than six thousand and five hundred spoken languages in the old world," Tama said.

"That many?" Kevin's eyes widened in surprise.

Before Tama could give them more historical facts, the back door swung open.

"Let's get this party started!" Bob bellowed as he pushed a cart full of juicy meats toward the canopy.

Helena, Simon, and a group of excited servants also followed with savory dishes and desserts. Overwhelmed with multiple surprises and an enormous amount of excitement, Canti clapped and jumped up and down.

"But I still don't understand. How did all of you know about this party? Especially you, Uncle," Canti said and eyed Kava suspiciously. "I only decided to have a party two days ago, that means you left Mars the very same day. Aren't you super busy in the Union?"

"Well, a certain someone had earnestly begged me to come. I couldn't turn down the request," Kava said and winked at Kevin, who blushed.

"I didn't beg."

"He even came to me for decoration advice," Queen Naraya chimed in. "So I let him borrow the runners and the chandelier."

"The tiny wireless lights run on solar power. Each light bulb has a tiny robot that can cling to any surface. It will take five men to remove it by force if you don't have access to the code that disables the robots," Kava explained. "It's the newest invention in Mars. These are only prototypes, though. Once they're developed, we can finally light up the Inter-Island Suspensions at night."

"Basically, Kevin asked us for help," King Edward interrupted before the conversation turned into another lengthy academic lecture. "He said you asked for a party, but he also wanted to make sure it was a surprise party for you."

"Young Master has really outdone himself this time, Little Miss," Bob hollered from the table as he cut and served the meats onto individual plates. "Please pardon me for saying this: I almost skinned him when he came to me with that outrageous request. Prepare a party in two days! But all is forgiven after he found me the best quality ingredients."

Canti gazed at Kevin, speechless.

"It's nothing," he stuttered. "Shall we dine now?"

Canti pounced on him and embraced him. "You're the best brother ever—"

Her weight made him stumble backward; he lost his

balance. Just then, Kevin remembered the lake right behind them.

Oh shoot.

The next thing he knew, coldness surrounded them as they submerged into darkness. Canti was still on top of him. She flailed and flapped her arms and legs wildly.

Not helpful.

When Kevin finally surfaced to the shore, dragging Canti alongside, he had no idea whether to scold her or to laugh with the others. They swam to the nearest rock.

Kevin swept the wet hair away from Canti's eyes and patted her back. "You okay?" he said as he panted. "Are you hurt? Did any of the water get into your—"

"Ack, ack...ha, ha. Hahahahaha!"

Kevin gawked at Canti, who was leaning against a rock and laughing uncontrollably.

"Me—Merry...Merry Christmas!" Canti said while shivering from the wetness and cold air, her wide grin tense and fixed on her face, with her teeth chattering.

Kevin couldn't help but snort and burst into laughter.

Helena helped them get dried and cleaned up, and then Kevin and Canti quickly rejoined the others. The party became brighter and merrier as the violet sky turned dark.

As he went to sleep that night, Kevin couldn't stop thinking about the food, the music, the laughter, and more importantly—the reunion of a family.

His heart ached and rejoiced at the same time. Someday, he would restore his empire and get his family back. But for now, he would cherish and enjoy every single moment he got to spend with the people here.

ABOUT THE AUTHOR

A.L. Rugova is an ordinary stay-at-home mom with three crazy kids and a doting husband. Her favorite leisure is daydreaming on the couch and singing in the kitchen. She is drawn to anything related to moon and autumn. Her family doesn't stay in one place long, so she's always looking forward to their next destination.

If you like this story, check out *The Free Prisoner* (Book One of TIAMIS series) and claim another deleted scene story for free. The rest of the series will be released in late 2020.

www.alrugova.com

Facebook: @rugovawrites
Twitter: @rugovawrites
Instagram: @rugovawrites

CRIMSON EYES

Urban Fantasy Poetry

ALICIA SCARBOROUGH

WHEN THE SNOW,
    Begins to fall,
    Watch the mice,
    Run for their halls,

In the winter,
    See them scurry,
    Watch as the mice,
    Hurry, hurry, hurry,

For the beast with the claws,
    Teeth and fur of white,
    Makes its appearance,
    During day and night,

See the mice,
    As they scatter,
    To save their lives,
    Like it matters,

The white creature,
    Sharp teeth and claws,
    Gather the mice,
    Within its jaws,

Snickersnack,
    Goes the neck and back,

By the cat, the cat, the cat,
With the crimson eyes,

In the storm of white,
    If one sees the color red,
    One is certain to be dead,
    By the cat, the cat, the cat,
    With the crimson eyes,

For the mice,
    In the winter,
    It is best,
    They do not venture,

For the cat, the cat, the cat,
    With the crimson eyes,
    Waits to strike,
    The unwary mice,
    And bring about their demise,

On the annual season,
    Of the cold,
    It is brought to reason,
    That each young mouse is told,

Do not venture,
    Into the falling ice,

For that is when,
Crimson eats the mice,

Several seasons,
    The mice did cower,
    Of the cat of white,
    With such power,

Until a young mouse,
    Of untold bravery,
    Took upon himself,
    To stop such tragedy,

Hunting the cat of white,
    And crimson eyes of red,
    This young mousy knight,
    Promised to strike it dead,

He ventured into the cold,
    Climbing snowy mountains,
    Until crimson eyes appeared,
    Looming and growling to instill the fear,

The young knight undeterred,
    Pulled forth his sword and with a blur,
    He swung and missed,
    The cat did hiss,

. . .

It swiped at the young knight,
    This creature of mousy lore,
    Only to be met by the young mouse's sword,
    Drawing vast amounts of bloody gore,

Crimson eyes,
    Loudly mewling,
    How could a mouse,
    Be so daring?

The knight of tiny height,
    Lunged again,
    The cat struck back,
    Snickersnack,
    They both attack,

Into the gloom,
    With Winter's howls,
    The mouse struck deep,
    Into Crimson's bowels,

It moaned and gapped,
    Wobbled and toppled,
    To the ground,
    It laid and grumbled,

Crimson wheezed,

Its final breath,
The mouse had slain it,
To its death,

No more do mice need to flee,
Upon the Winter's first freeze,
Instead they can stay outside,
And celebrate instead of hide,

The cat of white,
With the crimson eyes,
Was no longer,
A mouse's deadly surprise,

Free to play and scurry,
They have no need to,
Hurry, hurry, hurry,

For the cat, the cat, the cat,
With the crimson eyes,
Had been cut down to size,

Its crimson eyes faded,
Into the snow of white,
Its spirit haunting,
Every Winter's night,

. . .

The dying yowls,
> Carried by the Winter winds,
> Marked this beast's,
> Final End.

ABOUT THE AUTHOR

As a child, **Alicia Scarborough's** family would often find her acting out stories that she had envisioned for her toy ponies. Her mom and sisters admit that they would carefully sneak by her room to hear the conclusion of her riveting tales. Stories have always held a special place in Alicia's heart, and as she grew up, she continued to hone her craft. Alicia makes it a personal goal of hers to up the stakes with her characters every chance that she gets.

In her tween years Alicia grew up in the beautiful Sierra Mountains in the small town of Tehachapi, California. Because houses were far apart, a bike or car was necessary for visiting friends. So instead Alicia would use her imagination to come up with interesting stories to bide her time. By the time she was 13, her family moved and settled in Atlanta, Georgia, where she lives today.

Working full time as a Senior Product Engineer, Alicia's job involves using both technical and creative skills. On her off-hours she can be found drawing with charcoals, painting with watercolors, reading stories, writing, or learning new and interesting things.

www.charmed-embers-publications.com

Facebook: @aliciascarboroughauthor

Twitter: @foxglove1028
Instagram: @ally.scarborough
Bookbub: @alicia-scarborough

TROUBLE IN WINTER PARADISE

Cozy Mystery

MELANIE SNOW

Edited by
Qat Wanders

"Here, kitty, kitty!" I hear the tinkle of food hitting my bowl. I come running from my perch on the window ledge, where I am watching the village collect a new coat of snow.

"There you are, Zeva," Susie coos. She begins scratching that spot on my chin that makes me feel like I'm melting into a ball of love.

"I was watching the snow," I tell her.

"It's pretty, isn't it? We're in for a white winter wonderland!" Susie declares as she remembers the time she dropped her baking sheet when making kitty biscuits for Zeva. Susie thought she lost her ability to hear animals talk, but when Zeva shared her delight about living with her, Susie's ability resurfaced.

"I noticed that family moved in down the street—into the new Habitat for Humanity house you and Karen built."

"Yes, such nice people. It's a single mom, and her little girl is a darling."

"I don't know about her," I say testily.

Susie frowns. "Are you just reacting negatively to the change, or do you actually sense something?"

Susie knows me too well. "Something is off about her, Suze. I saw her standing in the yard, manipulating the snow."

"Manipulating it?" She furrows her brow. "Are you sure?"

"Sure as the snow is white."

"Do you think...she's gifted?" asks Susie

"I am positive she is."

Karen strides into the kitchen, twisting her left earring. "Hey, hun. Are you talking to the cat again?"

"Guilty as charged."

"I just don't know if this is normal. Lots of people love

their cats; they don't have actual conversations with them, though." Karen says as she pours herself a cup of coffee.

"Want me to make a souffle? I think today calls for a nice breakfast!"

"Save the special baking for the bakery today. We have to start Polly's winter party cake and we have at least a hundred cookies to bake," Karen replies. The two run Magical Incredible Delights Bakery, and the holiday season is their busiest time.

"I suppose," Susie sighs. "You know I could bake all day and still want to make you something special." She snuggles up to Karen for a morning kiss.

Karen softens and plants a firm kiss on her lips, squeezing her close. "I love you," she says. Her eyes reflect the deep love of her heart.

Then she reaches to pet me and I pull away, prancing out of the room.

"That cat still doesn't like me," she moans before grabbing her purse. "All right, let's go get 'em."

From my perch back on the windowsill, I watch them make their way down the slick sidewalk, holding hands. Neighbors wave at them from their yards. Some of the villagers still stare at them, but no one has ever boycotted their bakery or harassed them. I'll never forget the brick someone sent flying into our house back in Indiana. I can sense a person's bad intent from far away and I got plenty of bad vibes in our old home town.

It's not that I don't like Karen. I think she's really good for Susie. But... I lose my train of thought as a bird catches my attention. I watch it flit from branch to branch, my instincts taking over, the yearning to be outside in the snow chasing it overwhelming my senses.

My concentration is broken when the little girl comes back outside wearing a huge, ratty, red coat. She plays in the snow for a minute. Then she pauses, looking up at the flurry of soft white flakes drifting from the clouds.

A normal child would stick her tongue out, trying to taste the snow. But this little girl is anything but normal. With a self-assured motion of her hand, she sends the flakes whirling clockwise, then switches them to counterclockwise. She laughs at her control over the elements. She looks across the street, and her green eyes bore into me even through the window.

The hairs raise along my spine as I arch my back and hiss at her.

She just laughs. "I don't like you either," she says with her mind. Her telepathic voice is loud and clear.

I abandon my perch on the windowsill to hide in the closet. For the first time since landing in this little Vermont town, I sense trouble is coming our way.

Susie is exhausted, as she collapses on the couch. She drapes one hand over Karen's thigh and grabs a book with the other. She taught me to read last year, and I can make out the title: *Ruby Fruit Jungle* by Rita Mae Brown. Hmm. I curl up next to Susie and try to relax, but something is nagging at me.

"I can't believe all that we got done today," Karen finally says, breaking the comfortable silence that has settled over the living room, accompanied only by the sound of her news program playing at low volume. "We are going to sleep like babies!"

Susie smiles as she sets her book down for a moment. "I can't thank you enough for making this dream happen for me."

"It's my dream, too! Two successful lesbians, living in a New England mountain town without any trouble? I didn't even know this is what I wanted when I was getting my MBA at NYU, but it's everything I could have dreamed of and more."

"I'm just so happy." Susie snuggles deeper into Karen as Karen wraps a protective arm around her. Soon enough, Susie is asleep, her book falling into the couch crevice at her side. Karen gently rouses her and helps her to bed.

I join them after a much-needed visit to my food bowl. If I don't nibble on my food every half hour, I get really cranky.

"Would you like a treat?" Karen proffers a fish-flavored heart from a bottle next to her side of the bed. Always trying to bond with me, Karen gives me treats all the time. Susie is worried that I'm going to become diabetic, but who can resist that fish flavor? A bit guiltily, I accept the treat and then curl up between Susie's legs. Karen sighs, turns the light out, and goes to sleep. My own purring lulls me into a deep slumber soon after.

An image of the bakery fills my mind. It's dark, but I'm a cat, so my eyes can expertly make out the neat rows of cookies waiting to be set out in the display case tomorrow and the looming shape of a ten-tier cake. The smell of sugar is heavy in the air. The stillness of the shop is disrupted by a weird vibe, a sort of shrill through the empty space.

A blue portal opens, and the sense of a rift in the space-time continuum makes my hair stand on end. I see the neat rows of cookies lifting into the air, one by one, and then suddenly whooshing into the portal. Silently, the rest of the shop's contents lift up by themselves, and disappear into the vacuum. Muffins, croissants, cookies, slices of Italian wedding cake and carrot cake and spice cake. Those apple fritters Susie is so proud of. Suddenly all gone.

I don't like you either! echoes in my mind.

"Susie?"

"Yes, Zeva?" I feel my body go limp as she begins to scratch under my chin.

"Don't do that. It distracts me," I protest.

"What's wrong?" She trembles and pulls her hand away. "I can tell something is wrong."

I love Susie's intuition. When I first decided to speak to her five years ago, I thought she would fail to hear me, like all the humans who had had me before. Many of them wouldn't listen to me, yet they swore up and down weird things happened around me. That's why I kept going back to the shelter, to that dreadful kitty room! The other cats weren't like me, and they hissed at me like I was a ghost.

I was sure Susie would simply repeat the pattern. But instead, Susie dropped her baking sheet and stared at me. "This hasn't happened since I was a kid! Say it again?"

"I'm Zeva, and your house is okay. I would prefer easier access to the windowsills, though."

"Zeva! I was trying to find a name. Looks like you already have one." She then reached under my chin to scratch me, and I was in love.

From then on, she listened to every word I said. She took my advice when I told her to send Ned, a ghost of an old WWII veteran in the bedroom, to the other side. She listened to me when I told her who threw the brick into her living room, and then she had him apprehended by the cops. And when the local bank was robbed, I told her who did it, and she creatively found a way to turn in the perp without drawing suspicion to herself. Together, we had beat many criminals, and we had formed a paranormal investigation team, where I detect malevolent spirits in houses, and Susie sends them packing. Karen doesn't know about it, but we still do it when we get the calling. We just haven't had many callings since moving here.

"I had a dream," I tell Susie.

"What happened?"

"I think you've been robbed."

"Robbed?" She frantically looks around the house.

"Y—Yes—" I am cut off when Karen enters the kitchen. Karen is good for Susie, but her pronounced lack of belief in the paranormal has driven a wedge between Susie and me. Communication is much more difficult when she's around.

"Karen! We've been robbed!"

"Robbed?" Karen freezes, scanning the house. "I don't see anything missing."

"Was it at the bakery?" Susie asks me. Her eyes start welling up with tears. She knows better than to doubt anything I tell her.

"Yes," I reply.

"We have to get to the bakery now!" Susie shouts. She throws on her coat and runs out the door.

Karen shoots me a weird look before throwing on her own coat and chasing after Susie.

Susie is beside herself. They closed the bakery for the day and now sit on the couch as they chat with Sergeant Mike. I like Sergeant Mike's smell: warm coffee, starch, spicy aftershave.

I rub against his leg, and he smiles at me, offering the occasional scratch. I love the well of happiness I give people. Susie often takes me to the nursing home to cheer up the residents, and their sadness dissipates when I rub up on them.

"I don't know what we're supposed to do. That was thousands of dollars of goods...just gone," Karen shouts.

"What I find odd is that there's no sign of forced entry. Nothing on the security cameras. There was a strange blip in the feed around 3 a.m., and then the baked goods were gone when the footage resumed," Sergeant Mike shakes his head with disbelief.

"How can that happen?" Karen demands. "Did they hack our camera system or something?"

"Possibly. I've honestly never seen anything like this before," said Sergeant Mike, shaking his head with disbelief.

"It was the girl, and she created a portal," I told Susie. Now I could sense Susie's confusion. She was trying to figure out how to tell Sergeant Mike what she knew without garnering too many questions.

"I have a suspicion of who did it," Susie finally ventures.

Karen fixes her with a sharp glare. "Well, that information would be helpful right now!"

Susie sighs and leans forward, making a tent with her fingers. The lines on her forehead are pronounced as she cautiously selects her words. "Isabel and her little girl, Claire—they just moved in, and they don't have anything."

Sergeant Mike leans back against the couch, his eyebrows raised. He is no longer scratching me, so I decide to rub harder against his leg, leaving behind lots of little white hairs against the crisp dark blue of his pant leg. Now every cat in town will know that I am his favorite.

"You think they did it?" he asks.

"It's only a hunch." Susie shrugs her shoulders and almost reaches her ears. "I was thinking about going over and asking them if they knew anything."

"How would they have gotten into the shop and manipulated the camera footage?"

"That I have no idea about. Like I said, it's only a suspicion."

He sighs heavily. "Well, I'm happy to go talk to them, but I would absolutely hate to point fingers at innocent people. They are newcomers, and we want to make them feel welcome."

"That's why I'd like to handle it. It won't look as bad if I do it, and I'll be very tactful."

"I can't encourage you to do this on your own. I think I should at least accompany you. No one takes too kindly to an accusation of theft," Sergeant Mike suggests.

"This is insane! You can't just go accusing random people. How do you even know it's them?" Karen fires back.

"I just get those feelings, you know?" Susie says as she places her hands on her hips.

Karen then looks at me. She is well aware of the feelings Susie is talking about.

"I have to take Zeva with me," Susie adds, indicating to me.

Sergeant Mike smiles down at me. "I could see how Zeva would be helpful. Well, if you want to go over there now, I see Isabel's car in the driveway. I've been meaning to go say hi and meet them, anyway."

Karen says with confusion. "What is going on?" she mouths at Susie, as Susie tucks me under her arm to carry me across the street.

"Zeva told me," Susie mouths back.

Karen throws her hands up. "Well, I'm staying here. I have to figure out a plan to recover our losses."

"Okay." Susie plants a kiss on her forehead. "I love you."

As we near the house, Susie helped build for the single mom and her supernatural daughter, I feel queasy. The power of the little girl can be keenly felt several yards away, like a dull throb of intense energy.

Isabel opens the door. Confused, she welcomes Susie and Sergeant Mike inside. "Claire!" she calls. "We have company! Susie brought her kitty for you to play with."

"We just wanted to stop by and welcome you to the neighborhood," Sergeant Mike begins. I can feel his deep discomfort. "I'm the municipal police sergeant."

"How nice," Isabel beams. She gives them seats in her bare kitchen. "Um, I don't have much to offer you drink-wise...."

"That's fine. I already had coffee."

I notice his eyes lingering on Isabel for a second, and then he looks away, blushing. A feeling of warmth spreads through his aura. He likes her!

Isabel catches his glance and falters. "Um, well, it's really nice to meet you, Sergeant Mike."

As Claire enters the room, her piercing eyes land on the

policeman, and then her eyes penetrate mine. My skin prickles as she scoops me up.

"Be nice," Susie murmurs to me.

"Always," I grumble back, not hiding my sarcasm.

"Aren't you a nice kitty?" Isabel coos.

Claire nods. "I'm going to show him my room."

"Be careful," her mom's soothing voice warns.

Claire carries me back to her room. I would guess she is about ten, very little, and she carries me in that awkward way kids always do that leaves my back legs dangling and pinches some of my hair. I want to scratch her and run away, but that's against my nature.

"Here we go." She plops me on the quilt covering her bed. "I know why you're here," she adds pointedly.

"I know what you did," I reply.

"I'm not giving any of it back."

"Why would you use your powers to do something bad like that?"

She shrugs. "My mom was crying that she doesn't have any food for a nice Christmas. So, I got her enough to have a party! She can invite everyone over now."

"You think people won't realize where the baked goods are from? This is a small town, Claire. Susie will definitely know, if no one else does."

"I haven't worked that part out," Claire muses while her eyes dance around the room. "Maybe I can change the goods into other things, so no one knows where they came from. I know I can do it, but I have to figure out how."

"How are you planning to explain to your mom how you got all that stuff, anyway? Won't you get into trouble?" I attempt to reason with her.

"My mom is used to people giving me things. I'm cute."

"She has no idea what you can do, does she?"

"The fewer people who know, the better. You better not tattle on me."

"I already did. Susie knows it's you." I lay down and curl up, enjoying the sensation of her quilt. "You have to come clean. You have to give that stuff back."

"Why would I do that?" She laughs. "It's mine now."

I send her a feeling of Susie's despair and distress. I see her deflate a bit. The mean glint in her eye fades, and I can see the fragility of her ten-year-old soul shining through the bright green of her pupils.

"That's why," I explain. "Do you really want to use your gift to make people feel like that?"

"But what about me? What about my mom?" She sends back a memory of her mom sobbing in a sparsely furnished living room while snow falls outside the window. "That was last winter. She signed me up for Toys for Tots, but she couldn't even afford a tree. And we see all these people with their decorations and their parties, and we can't have any of it."

"What if we gave you and your mom the winter party of a lifetime? What if we brought baked goods and had people over?" I suggest. I envision the perfect winter party, with villagers packed into the tiny rooms and a beautiful tree twinkling in the living room, overflowing with presents underneath. "Everyone would bring food and gifts."

Claire hesitates, relishing the image I'm sending into her mind. "Nobody has ever come over for a party at our house. And I've never had that many presents."

"Susie will make it happen. She really likes you guys. But she's hurt right now, and only you can make it right."

"What if I get into trouble?"

"Just show me where the goods are, and I'll take care of

the rest. You won't get into trouble. No one will know you did it but you, me, and Susie," I assure her.

With a shivering body, she sends me an image of a little hunting cabin down by the river. The baked goods are all lined up on the floor, nestled inside in their plastic wrap, frigid and waiting to be snarfed.

"Thank you," I tell her. I give her a little nudge. "You don't like me because you know I can see through you."

"I still don't know if I will ever like you."—wiping tears from her cheeks—"You won't come back. You won't give us that party. I've been let down before."

"Watch me." I hop off the bed and trot back into the kitchen. Sergeant Mike is engaged in deep conversation with Isabel, and Isabel's cheeks are red as she takes in his muscular figure, defined by the crisp dark blue lines of his uniform. Susie sits there awkwardly, waiting for me to finish my chat with Claire. She hasn't said anything about the robbery to Isabel yet.

"I know where the backed goods are," I inform Susie. "We have to act fast before Claire changes her mind and moves them somewhere else. Are you coming with me Susie?".

"Uh, actually, I think I'm going to go. I have to get back to Karen. We got robbed today, and we are dealing with the aftermath." Susie says hurriedly, scooping me up.

"Oh, no!" Isabel cries. "That's terrible. Is there anything I can do?"

Sergeant Mike shifts in his seat. "Would you happen to know—"

"I have it handled," Susie cuts him off with a bright smile. "I know where all of the goods are, and I'm going to go recover them before I go back to the bakery to get Karen. Thanks for your hospitality!"

Sergeant Mike looks taken aback. "You do know?"

"Yes." She shoots him a wink before darting out the door. He simply stares after her, stunned.

Karen helps us retrieve the goods from the cabin. "This is just outlandish. I don't understand any of this," she repeats over and over.

"You don't understand Zeva's powers. I've been trying to find a way to tell you, but I was scared you would think I was crazy and bolt. I mean, any rational person would," Susie apologizes. "Now you see the proof."

"I mean...." Karen stops to stare at me. "I guess this is pretty irrefutable proof, but my rational mind can't comprehend any of it."

"Zeva has a special ability.... A psychic ability, really. And I have the ability to talk to animals. I've had it since I was a kid. Since I got Zeva, we have had a connection...and she solves mysteries." Susie lets out a little laugh. "We've solved bank robberies; we've conducted paranormal investigations; we've done it all. She does the sleuthing, and I interpret the results."

"How are we going to explain that to Sergeant Mike? He's going to want to know how we found this stuff."

"I usually don't offer a real explanation. After all, I don't want to get locked up in a looney bin!"

"But what about the girl? How on Earth did she break into our shop, move all these goods, and then erase the camera footage? The mom has to be involved. Heck, a whole team would have to be involved to accomplish all that!" Karen exclaims, waving her arms at the mounds of goods piled in the back seat of her SUV.

"The girl is also...special. Zeva sensed it when she first saw the girl playing outside. Claire used her powers to create a wormhole, so to speak, between the bakery and this cabin. The warp in the space-time continuum messed with the camera footage, making it lose time," Susie explains, as if it's the most logical thing in the world. "I've seen it before, but that girl is unbelievably powerful! For an untrained gift, she is eerily talented at using it."

Karen doesn't say anything more. Susie and I let it sink in for her.

"We still have a problem," Karen finally pipes up when we finished retrieving all the goods. "This can't be sanitary." She indicates the rough-board floor of the little cabin. "We're going to have to remake all of these before we sell them, so we still lose a lot of money."

"Easy, use the girl's powers," I say.

Susie smiles at me, then says to Karen, "We'll find a way, okay?"

Karen just glances at me and back to Susie, then nods. "Okay. I'm going to leave this up to you two witches then."

Susie and I laugh to myself. Karen is finally on board!

That night, I cuddle with Karen after she gives me my customary treat. She stares at me for a minute before she starts rubbing my ears. "Good kitty?" she says.

I blink my eyes at her before tucking into a ball and going to sleep. She stays awake for a while, attempting to make sense of it all, before finally giving up and falling asleep herself.

"Well, I see you recovered everything." Sergeant Mike skeptically takes in the neat rows of pastries, cookies, and cakes in the bakery.

I sit on my perch on the counter. While my presence in the bakery poses a sanitation issue, the customers adore me. Susie sometimes allows me to come in to drive sales. I relish all the pets and coos I get whenever I preside the counter. The only rule is that I can't step on the equipment or the display trays.

"Yep! We figured it all out." Susie is running around the bakery more than usual. "What can I get for you today?"

Sergeant Mike blinks at her. Then he points to some sugar cookies cut in the shapes of snowflakes and stars. "I want a dozen sugar cookies. All different shapes, please."

"Are you going to eat all these before lunch?" Karen jokes as she hunches over the books at her little desk in the corner.

"Actually, I'm taking them to Isabel and Claire. I'm taking Isabel out to dinner tonight, and I wanted to leave Claire something to munch on while the sitter watches her."

"Oh!" Susie beams. "So, you two hit it off?"

"Yeah, I don't know what it is about her, but I just really like her. We have great conversations, and I feel like she gets me—like actually gets me."

I look over at Susie and Karen and catch them in a state of beaming delight from the news.

"I've been going by to visit them every day. I don't think Claire cares for me much, though." Sergeant Mike frowns, his energy turning sad.

"She just has to get used to you. Did Isabel tell you about the party?" Susie finishes bagging up the cookies and rings them up.

"Yeah, she's really excited about it. She says she has never hosted a party in her life, and she can't believe how nice everyone in this town is. I hope we've made her feel welcome. She's had a rough go of things for a long time."

Sergeant Mike happily accepts the bag of cookies. He glances at me and gives me a smile. "So, who robbed you?"

Susie sighs. She was hoping he wouldn't circle back to that subject. "I would prefer not to say. I don't want to get anyone in trouble. Someone confessed and told me where the goods were stashed. Save for a few cookies the culprit had snacked on, everything was returned to us. So, hopefully, you understand that I don't want to mention any names."

"Fair enough." Mike pats the bag of cookies, then gives me a final scratch on my neck. "It makes my paperwork more complicated, but I prefer not getting people in trouble, either, as long as they do the right thing in the end. Well, I'm glad everything worked out. See you at the party."

"Enjoy your date! You're going to make Isabel and Claire very happy," Susie calls after him.

"You are an adept liar. You never lie directly, and that's how you get away with it," Karen comments, after the door jingles shut behind Sergeant Mike.

Susie sighs and sits on the edge of Karen's desk. "It just comes with the territory. I'm sorry I lied to you for so long, but I didn't want you to think I was crazy."

"Honestly, I already thought something was off when you would carry on long conversations with the cat, as if she was talking back to you!" Karen laughs and leans up to give Susie a kiss. "I always knew you were magical. I just didn't think literally!"

"Aw, stop it," Susie blushes. "I love you to the moon and back."

"I love you more than the whole world," Karen coos back.

❄

"See? I told you to trust me," I tell Claire at the party.

It is Saturday, and the snow is falling, collecting in big heaps outside. The house is filled with cheer as people laugh and mingle in the living room and the narrow kitchen. The rich aroma of hot chocolate and the huge vanilla cream cake with its fondant snowman on top makes my nostrils tingle.

Polly donated the cake from her own winter party, and Susie delivered it earlier in the day, along with dozens of sugar cookies and leaf-shaped lady fingers that she and Karen donated from the bakery.

"I've never been so happy before," Claire replies. She fingers a string of lights that the town donated to decorate the modest house's tree. "I want to open a present already."

"You have to wait until midnight," I joke.

"All of you guys are the best." She smiles as she scratches me. "I guess I do like you."

"I'm pretty likable." I arch my back into her hand, enjoying the tender way she pets my white fur. "Now you need to start liking Sergeant Mike."

"Every time my mom dates someone, she gets her heart broken. I have to hug her for days because she won't stop crying."

"Sergeant Mike isn't like that, I promise you. I feel real love in his heart whenever he looks at your mom." I gaze across the room at Mike and Isabel cuddling on the couch. Isabel's cheeks are strained because she is smiling so much.

Claire smiles for a quick moment then grimaces. "They're kind of gross. They're always kissing. Ew!"

"You'll get used to it. One day, you'll be kissing up on somebody like that, too."

I watch Susie and Karen holding hands as they talk to other villagers. They glow with happiness; Susie's cheeks are ruddy from the wine she's drinking which also makes her body ripple when she giggles.

"Hey, do you want to play?" A little girl named Cassie walks up to Claire. Claire is standing alone by the tree, reaching down to touch my head as I sit at her feet. She is able to talk to me telepathically, unlike Susie, so she looks as if she is just standing by herself with no one to talk to.

"Sure," Claire says shyly.

The girl smiles and takes Clarie's hand. The two run off to join the other children, who are playing in the hallway. Claire glances back at me for a second and smiles. I've never seen her smile like that before. I twitch my tail and blink my eyes, letting her know that I'm happy, too.

ABOUT THE AUTHOR

Melanie Snow is an author and introverted eclectic witch. She has an insatiable passion for nature, animals, and the exploration into the artes of her ancestors. She deems truth in magic, faeries, talking animals, and spirit guides. Melanie weaves her true life adventures into her stories. Her books have been published by Spirit Paw Press, LLC.

https://wendyvandepoll.com/melanie-snow

Facebook: @melaniesnow.cozymysteries
Instagram: @melaniesnow.cozymysteries

NINTH LIFE

Dark Urban Fantasy

QATARINA WANDERS

Edited by
Rachel McCracken

Proofread by
Allison Goddard

NIKKI ALBRIGHT GASPED as she came to. You would think that after rising from the dead eight times, she would have gotten used to the experience.

No.

Because first of all, she had died as a little white house cat. And when she died in that form, she transformed back to a human after a while. Waking up in human form, after dying as a cat, had a way of screwing with one's mind.

So when Nikki jerked awake, she felt like she had been removed from one body and deposited haphazardly in another. She felt totally wronged. Violated. Goosebumps popped up all over her body.

Nikki shivered, trying to calm her mind. She was on the verge of panic. But it wasn't because of the way she felt *mentally*. It was because of the way she felt *physically*.

Freezing cold.

It could only mean one thing: winter.

Nikki finally opened her eyes and found herself half buried in snow, surrounded by a hilly area. The trees around her were sparse, and most of them were void of leaves. It was dark, and there was a highway somewhere down to her right. She knew this because of the intermittent rush of passing vehicles.

Her whole body was numb. It wasn't a miracle that she hadn't died of frostbite already, because she knew she'd been in the ice for as long as it had been snowing. No, it was no miracle that she could still move her toes and fingers or wiggle her nose. It was the magic coursing through her body —that and the fact that she'd died for the eighth time and had come back to life.

She was now on her ninth life.

Her very last one.

The first thing Nikki did, after she dug herself out of the

five-inch-deep snow she'd been partially buried under, was try to calm her racing heart.

The truth was, she was terrified. Because she knew that if she died now, she was never coming back. She was going to stay dead, and that would be it. No more Nikki. No more sweet teenage girl. No more prized member of the high school cheerleading squad. No more. The very concept of dying and staying dead was very foreign to her, and it made her feel exposed.

Nikki felt like death hovered over her, because all the time she'd known that she had nine lives, she had lived freely—if not recklessly. And it wasn't as though she'd died a couple of times from living carelessly. No, it was the damn dark elf—her nemesis. It was he who had killed her eight times—no, seven. The eighth one had been during the crisis in New Haven with the bottomless pit opening, and the Beast, and all of Hell's host pouring onto the earth.

With that one, she had tried to help, and she had been picked up in her housecat form and carried all the way out of New Haven and dropped to her death. But that was in the fall, several months ago.

She had been dead for several months? Usually, she resurrected within hours—the first time, actually, she had gasped back to life after only a few minutes. But the fewer lives she had, the more time it took her to resurrect. The last time before this, she'd been gone for over a week.

This time, it was unprecedented. She had been dead for months—although it only felt like a moment. But the snow all around her was proof.

Look at the silver lining, she said to herself. *At least the world hasn't ended.*

Nikki grunted as she pulled herself to her feet. She felt shudder after shudder of pain as her joints snapped out of misalignment, and knotted muscles unknotted themselves. She shut her eyes and breathed away the pain, stretching herself to get all the kinks out.

Weirdly, she didn't feel hungry or famished. She felt normal, although weakened by the lack of activity.

Nikki knew that if she had stayed dead for months, it meant this really was her last life. Her ninth life. If she died now, she was headed straight for the upper room.

The thought caused another shudder to rip through her spine.

Nikki had never really been one to fear death. But now it was different. Now she was grappling with it. With existentialism. With what was beyond the veil of death. All the times she'd died, she had woken up, and it had felt like she'd been gone for only a second. Even now that she'd obviously been dead for months.

Was that what death was like? A whole bunch of nothing? Would she just cease to exist? What was inexistence like?

Nikki shivered again. This time it wasn't because of the terror permeating the fiber of her being. It was because the cold was finally starting to get to her. She was wearing a brown leather jacket over a white top and blue jeans. She was also sporting cowboy boots. Not really the best snow attire. The cold was already penetrating into her bones.

Now that she was alive, if she stayed in the freezing cold for much longer, she was definitely going to get frostbite and probably freeze to death.

Gently, she made her way toward the sound of passing cars. From time to time, she used the cold, tall, eerie trees as support. Because she hadn't walked for the last several months, her legs were weak and wobbling.

The only light that guided her down the rough terrain of

the mountainside emanated from the starry skies and the powerful glow of the moon. Although it did terrify her when she heard the sound of owls in the trees. She just hoped she didn't run into a nasty supernatural that prowled the mountains at night or a group of vampires skulking around the trees at this hour.

Nikki looked up at the moon. Right. It was full. Just splendid. So add werewolves to the list of supernaturals that would find her sumptuous flesh enticing.

Hobbling up the hill, she made it to the highway with only a sprained ankle. She recognized the highway. It was the one that led right into New Haven. At this time, it was totally dark and void of any cars. Looking around, she found a large rock to sit on by the shoulder of the road. Making herself as comfortable as possible, she tightened her clothing and rubbed her palms together, trying to generate warmth.

It wasn't snowing, but it felt like it had snowed not too long ago. The air felt like icicles every time she inhaled.

As Nikki sat on the roadside, she did her best to swallow the fear threatening to take over her body. Every little sound had her turning around to see who or what it was. When she wasn't overcome by fright, she was thinking about how New Haven was doing now.

She wondered how they had won against the Beast and the evil magician. Because at the time when she had been attacked by a winged creature and brought out here to be killed, it seemed as though they had been losing to them. Nikki had joined the fight not only because supernaturals were outlawed in New Haven—and she and her family were among the secret supernaturals living there—but also because she believed in the cause. She had wanted to help.

When Nikki had tried to persuade her parents to join

her, they had vehemently refused, claiming that if they survived the fight and won, they would be ostracized. Humans had no capacity for forgiveness when it came to supernaturals, they had told her.

Of course, being strong willed, she ran off to help anyway, and then *BOOM!* She was picked off by a winged creature and . . . well, you know the rest of the story.

For months, she had been missing from home. She wondered what her parents thought had happened to her. Maybe they thought she was a casualty of the war between the world of the living and the world of the dead. Maybe they'd think she ran off or something.

Nikki wondered what had happened to the evil magician. She wondered how they had won the war. Because they had obviously won. The world was still intact, after all.

Time flew by while she sat there rubbing her palms together and trying to stay alive. Soon enough, a flatbed approached, heading in the direction of Dallas. With a loud squeak, Nikki flew off the rock and ran straight into the road, which was something she would normally do when she had a couple of lives to spare.

Then it slammed into her mind that she was on her ninth life, and just like that, she scampered back to the side of the road.

The flatbed driver had seen her, however, so he slowed to a stop right next to her. Nikki peered into the truck and saw a round-faced man. Elderly and fatherly. He looked at her with compassion. "What are you doing out here all by yourself on Christmas Eve?" he asked.

Nikki felt her brows furrow of their own accord. "Christmas Eve . . . ?" she stuttered, her mind spinning. She'd been buried under the ice for *four months*?

The man in the truck looked at her quizzically. She

could tell he was trying to decide whether it was safe to admit her into his car. He looked behind her at the mountain, his eyes roaming about in search of signs of . . . who knew what?

"Yes, it's Christmas Eve," the man finally said. "Would you like a ride into town? Do your parents know you're out here all by yourself?"

Nikki knew that her stuttering was becoming more suspicious. But the thing was, she couldn't help herself. Four months. She'd been dead for *four months*.

"Hello?" The man snapped her back to reality.

She blinked at him. She couldn't remember what question he had asked, so she blurted out, "I need to get to New Haven. My parents live there."

"Well, you're in luck, because I got supplies to deliver to the local mart there." With a big smile, the man offered kindly, "Come on. Hop in."

Without thinking, Nikki went around the front of the cab and climbed into the passenger seat, but not before spying the crates of soda on the back of the flatbed.

The moment she was in, the man started fidgeting with things in the cab, trying to make her more comfortable. He wound up all the windows and put the heater on full blast. He was gracious enough not to engage her in any conversation for the first half of their journey, allowing her to thaw first. The ice hidden in all parts of her clothes melted first, wetting her body.

The heat kept blasting at her until her bones were back to normal and she wasn't shivering or shuddering. Then the warmth began to comfort her. Her thinking returned to normal. She was no longer in survival mode. All of a sudden, she was happy to be alive. Grateful she was being driven back to her town.

Yeah, she was on her ninth life. Okay. It certainly wasn't the end. There were lots of people who weren't supernatural like she was, yet they lived to old ages. If she just forgot that she was a supernatural and lived a normal life like her parents—who were on their ninth lives as well—she would live to a ripe old age.

Nikki sat with that thought to the extent that she started to smile. She decided she was happy with herself. Even, she was expectant to get home. She wondered about the vigilantes and the anti-supernatural laws. Had New Haven changed since she was gone? Since the Beast came out of the bottomless pit, and all the supernaturals came into the open and helped fight the Beast, she supposed the law might have been repealed. Or not. With humans, you never could tell.

"You seem happy enough," said the man to her left.

Nikki flinched at the man's husky voice. She had almost forgotten he was there, driving the truck.

He waited for a response, but she had none, particularly because he hadn't asked a question.

Finally, the man cleared his throat. "Where in New Haven do you live? I can drop you off before heading to the mart.

"I live on Main Street," she replied in a heartbeat.

"I suppose you didn't hear about that house that burned down there in the fall?"

Nikki didn't reply. The truth was, she *had* heard of it. It had been burned down thanks to her cheerleading captain, Emily, who was apparently also a powerful owl shifter. The house had belonged to a family of evil magicians, and Emily had come to rescue her friends who were being held there or something. However, Nikki wasn't going to say all these things to someone who was obviously an absolute stranger to the little town of New Haven.

So she did what she always did when she was asked questions that pertained to supernaturals. She remained silent. It was a protocol she started to follow when she realized she wasn't normal like others. She had been told by her parents to keep silent when supernatural topics came up. That way she wouldn't say anything that could implicate her and bring on the scrutinizing eyes of the vigilante task force.

After a while, the man asked, "You don't talk much, do you?"

Nikki didn't reply to that one either.

They drove into New Haven in silence. Nikki kept her eyes peeled to observe changes. At the time she had left, a war had almost torn the town into two. She was keen to see if there would be signs of the war.

She didn't see any.

They drove through the thick of the town. All she saw was snow, Christmas trees, Christmas lights, and lots of merrymaking. The streets were filled with people, even at this late in the night. It was as though the entire town was waiting for Christmas Day.

"What time is it?" Nikki croaked, her heart already beating as they approached Main Street.

"A little after eleven," said the man.

Nikki frowned. The energy in the town was high. Almost everywhere they passed, she saw people. New Haven had come out in force to celebrate Christmas Eve.

Also, she saw no sign of destruction. Even the town center had been repaired. It had to have involved magic. Either that, or the town's administrative team was very efficient. But Nikki would go with magic and sorcery any time, any day.

The man pulled off the main road that snaked through New Haven like a back bone. He didn't turn into the road that would lead to Main Street. He parked at the mouth of the road instead. There was a barbecue and a knot of people hanging around, laughing.

"You'll be okay?" the man asked after Nikki climbed down.

"Sure," Nikki said. "Thanks." With that, she turned her back on the man and walked down the street.

She could feel the man's eyes on the back of her head as she stalked into the street. After a while, she heard the engine rev and the tires screech back onto the main road. Then she turned and saw that the man's flatbed had gone.

Nikki turned onto Main Street, and it was as though everything shifted from cheeriness to depression. The avenue was completely abandoned and felt cold. Only a few houses had Christmas lights decorating their frontage. She walked to the fourth house from the mouth of the street—the house on the right. She paused in front, and looked down the street to the ruin that had once been the Alfred mansion.

Nikki could remember the day the house had been razed to the ground. It had been one of the most terrifying periods of their lives, because after the incident, the vigilantes had questioned everyone, looking for the supernatural elements that had caused the fire.

She returned her attention to the house. *Her* house. Her heart beat heavily in her chest. She wondered what she would say. She knew her parents would be heartbroken that she had lost her eighth life and was now on her ninth. Being a cat shifter was a blessing, especially when you knew you had eight passes on death. But now she had lost those eight —seven of which she had lost battling the dark elf, and the

ninth she had lost battling a winged creature from hell—
and while it was quite an exciting campfire story, it would
devastate her parents.

"Maybe I should walk away . . . ," Nikki thought aloud.

"Yes. Maybe you should."

Nikki stiffened. She knew that voice. It was the voice of
death. The dark elf.

Before she could react, she felt the dark elf move. She
swiveled around, but there was nothing she could do. The
fae creature of darkness had its sword swinging toward her
chest already. She only had enough time to let out a guttural
scream as the magical sword plunged right into her heart
and out her back.

Nikki felt her ninth life slide out her body into the
sword. All she saw in her moment of death was the fiery
eyes of the evil fae, his gaze filled with hatred. The last
thought to cross her mind, as she collapsed to her knees,
was *what had she done to deserve such animosity?*

As the dark elf yanked out its sword, the young cat
shifter—Nikki Albright—collapsed to the ground, dead.

Light exploded all around. The fae creature shielded his
eyes. When the light receded, Nikki Albright's eyes opened.
That was when she knew she shouldn't be alive. She was as
shocked as the elf.

But something was different. *She* was ... well, different.

Nikki frowned as she pulled herself to her feet and
looked down at herself. Standing before the evil creature,
she had no fear. Nothing.

The snow began to fall hard again.

She looked up at the dark elf, every fiber of her being

suffused with powerful shifter magic. But it was not a house cat. It was something else. *She* was something else.

The elf snarled and raised his sword. This time, Nikki ran toward him. She leaped—there was another glorious flash of powerful beams of light—and when she erupted out of the light, she was no longer human.

She was a huge white mountain lion.

The dark elf saw this and turned to run. But Nikki Albright—aka Mountain Lion—pounced on him and tore the creature to pieces, scattering his carcass across the street. Then she roared—a splitting roar that caused the houses and the street to rumble.

Moments later, she transformed back to her human self.

What the heck just happened???

Someone applauded.

Nikki turned to see her mom and dad standing in the doorway. She glanced at them in disbelief. "You knew?"

"What? That you were alive all this time or that when you lost your ninth life, your true nature as a mountain lion would come forth?" asked Mom so casually one would think the woman was merely asking what her daughter wanted for dinner.

Nikki didn't know what to say, so she stood in silence.

Dad spoke this time. "Why don't you come on in, and we'll tell you more about our family heritage?"

Without sparing another glance to the dark elf's shriveling carcass, Nikki stepped inside her home with her parents, anxious to learn about her dual nature.

ABOUT THE AUTHOR

Qatarina Wanders is a former circus performer turned author with a unicorn and pug obsession. When she isn't writing or editing books about unicorns or pugs (or cat shifters, vampires, werewolves, faeries, witches, angels, or succubi), she is likely eating sushi with her daughter or jumping out of a plane in the Rocky Mountains.

If you enjoyed Nikki's story, and you would like to read more about the destruction that took place in New Haven, you can check out *Adopted by the Owl*, Book One of the *Owl Shifter Chronicles*. It tells the story of Nikki's cheerleading captain, Emily the owl shifter, and the family of evil magicians.

www.wanderingwordsmedia.com

Facebook: @qatwrites
Instagram: @qatwanders
Pinterest: @qatwanders
Amazon: @qatarinawanders

Made in United States
Orlando, FL
09 February 2024